Evil N

A Max

By Rick Haynes

Best Wishes
Rich
xxx

RICK HAYNES

Evil Never Dies

A Maxilla Story

http://profnexus.wix.com/rickhaynes

Edited by Alex Roddie
Pinnacle Editorial
www.pinnacleeditorial.co.uk

Evil Never Dies
Copyright © Rick Haynes 2015

CREATESPACE EDITION

Rick Haynes asserts the moral right to be identified as the author of this work.

ALL RIGHTS RESERVED

All of the characters, names and organisations in these stories are fictitious and are the work of the author's imagination. Any resemblance to actual persons, events or organisations, either living or dead, is entirely coincidental.

All rights reserved. No part of this publication may be reproduced, stored in a retrieval system, or transmitted in any form or by any other means, electronic, mechanical, photocopying, recording or otherwise, without the prior written permission of the author.

TABLE OF CONTENTS

Dedication	1
Acknowledgements	2
Foreword	3
Evil Never Dies	
The Prologue	5
Chapter 1	9
Chapter 2	21
Chapter 3	27
Chapter 4	47
Chapter 5	49
Chapter 6	62
Chapter 7	79
Chapter 8	100
Chapter 9	123
Chapter 10	133
Chapter 11	139
Chapter 12	143
Chapter 13	146
Chapter 14	148
Chapter 15	150
Chapter 16	154
Chapter 17	165

Chapter 18	173
Chapter 19	179
Chapter 20	190
Chapter 21	200
Chapter 22	207
Chapter 23	217
Chapter 24	227
Chapter 25	230
Epilogue	232
About the Author	236
Future Projects	237

DEDICATION

This book is dedicated to my wonderful wife Teresa, for without her love, this book would never have seen the light of day, let alone been finished.

ACKNOWLEDGEMENTS

My grateful thanks go to my editor Alex Roddie. His superb editing skills and support have shown me the way.
http://www.pinnacleeditorial.co.uk
I would extend my thanks to Richard K Green, the designer of my amazing book cover.
http://www.richardkgreen.com
I would also like to thank the following for their work on my excellent YouTube video.
https://www.youtube.com/watch?v=RrO0UkG-ZWU&feature=youtu.be
Russell Carey – Composer.
Ryan Haynes – 2 Far South Productions – Video and Audio Final edit.
My thanks must also go to Carol Westron and Richard Bunce for their help and guidance.
And lastly a big thank you to my readers and all those supporting me.

FOREWORD

I have always enjoyed medieval fantasy tales. Once I started, I could never put them down, often reading them into the early hours. I found myself living the characters that jumped out from the pages. I always hoped that one day I could create my own world, full of vile creatures and true heroes. And after the passing of too many seasons I finally began to remove the ideas from my head and commence writing.

It has taken nearly 18 months to produce a story that had lain dormant for so many years. Evil Never Dies is my first novel and is a classic tale of good and evil set against a backdrop of green lands, snowy mountains and dusty plains.

I show the horrors of war, as well as the loyalty and fears of all those involved. I believe that all men are flawed, and I leave it to you, the reader, to decide whether I have succeeded in showing their strengths and weaknesses, their compassion and cruelty. For war brings out the best and the worst in even the gentlest of men.

I have let my mind wander freely over the words, and I hope that you will enjoy your trip into the world of my imagination.

Evil Never Dies
THE PROLOGUE

THE MOUNTAINS FORMED after the lands had been covered in fire, lava and ash. Ice had shaped valleys and the wind and rain had scoured the summits into jagged peaks. Immune to any hardship and interference, only the gods lived in such desolate places. From their lofty domain they looked down on the world of man.

On the lower slope of Mount Soar, a vast number of caves ran through the mountain. Deep and gloomy they served as scant protection for the few animals that dared to wander so high and as a refuge for the seldom seen humans.

Two men sat around a blazing fire in one of the upper caves. A copper pot boiled. One stirred the contents, looking hopeful that the meat would soon be cooked. He shivered constantly, his hand automatically stirring faster.

Long dark clothes swathed the other. A wide-brimmed floppy hat obscured his thin bony face, weathered by time. Yet everything about him was illusory, for he could sit naked in a snow drift and be unconcerned, whereas his companion would freeze in an instant without his help.

He loved the entertainment; humans were usually predictable, yet some could still surprise him. But he had learnt that the body of a frail old man always yielded the best results.

"What is your name, human?"

"Ernon … the lame. What should I call you … lord?"

"You, my cold friend … you may call me Titian. So, tell me what you want."

"I want power, to control them and take my revenge."

"Really?"

"Yes my lord. I have studied the dark side of magic and can readily proceed with the ten incantations."

"Yes! Yes! Admittedly, you have a talent for cruelty and minor magic otherwise you would not be sitting here, but are you ready to give up many years of your life to learn the secrets of the dark arts? The teaching never ceases, for as you learn you move on to the next level of understanding. But remember, if you fail, death is inevitable."

Looking at the frailty of the man stirring a hot stew did not fill Titian with any great confidence, but the mortal's eager nod swayed him.

"You will endure pain unlike any other as your mind is exposed and altered. Your body will shrink and grow as I deem fit. At some point you will fall on your knees and beg to die. By then, it will be too late. The gods will own you body and soul, and only they, will allow your demise. This is the point of no return, Ernon. Take it … or maybe freeze."

Titian watched Ernon, knowing the doubts that flooded his brain. He knew this mortal, knew that all his life he had been scorned by others. Lame-leg they would shout. Silently he had endured all the abuse but the hatred had festered. Titian was aware that physical pain had always been a part of Ernon's life; he would cope with it, but the mental anguish of this new challenge would be severe. Ernon had dreamed of a day of retribution for so long, but Titian saw him hesitate at the point of no return.

"I wish to learn my lord and be your faithful servant whatever the cost. I want … need …to repay my tormentors."

Hot blood surged through Titian's veins, and his face grew crimson with excitement. The thought of a new game sent shudders down his spine.

"As you wish but I must also warn you that your enemies will be as numerous as your friends. Men will take sides – they always do – but you can prevail. It will be a long hard road; are you ready?"

"Yes, my lord."

"Good! One more thing. The gods will also take sides."

Titian saw Ernon hesitate. He ignored the signs.

"I will use a sign as a medium for your energy. It will be used to control your allies and to strike fear into your enemies."

Flurries of future scenes raced through Titian's mind. The puny human would likely cause great havoc in the world below and he would rejoice in the fun, even though he risked the wrath of his parents Obsidian and Radiance.

"You will be known as Myracadonis the shaman. Now, let us begin," said Titian, the God of Fire.

CHAPTER 1

THE HELGS HAD marched from the mountains almost unseen. Usually a quiet nation, they had declared a sudden interest in war. A petty squabble over land had somehow grown into a major conflict in a matter of months. They had ridden southwards, driven by a manic desire, into the northern lands of the Stormborn and the Maxilla clans. Rumours spread about their savagery when they sacked distant farms. Those in the south feared for the future but doubted that any race could be as brutal as the stories suggested. They were wrong.

A small band of Temujin driving their horses across the north-western lands of the Maxilla also sent warnings to the south. The Helgs had murdered men, women, children and livestock, leaving burning farmsteads in their wake. They had butchered every animal, and sown salt into lush farm meadows. From the tracks, they estimated a travelling party of nearly five thousand Helgs, riding light and fast. The reports from the Temujin were taken more seriously. The enemy had travelled many miles in a short time.

Stormborn cavalry to the west would join forces with the Maxilla army, for it became clear that the home of the Maxilla would be the main target. Lightly-armed Temujin bowmen rode from the plains with many horses. Friends answered the call of friends. The Helgs had to be stopped, and the combined might of three nations should prove sufficient to complete the task. Alas the confidence of the defenders would soon be dented.

Refugees flooded towards Castle Stoke where King Leofrick sat on the throne of the Stormborn. As many of his troops had already left, the king ordered the farmers be added to the existing militia. He was not prepared to return to a ruin if the Helgs decided to change course.

Eighty miles to the north-east, Lord Bokin had charged his men with the protection of the Maxilla clan. His riders – some with light armour and broadsword, but most with leather jacket and spear – had ridden to await the attack of the Helgs from the west. He ordered the gates of Castle Bokin to close as soon as the second battle horn sounded. Estimating that the local villages held about four hundred of his people, he felt that the castle could hold them all, along with the permanent residents and two hundred fighting men left on guard. If only they had more time, he thought, for without the security of the stone walls some of his people would die, but he had no choice.

Only six miles separated the two armies when the huge host appeared on the western hills. The sound of the first war horn sent fear into the people streaming towards the castle. The old and the tardy would be too slow. Bokin joined his horsemen a few miles beyond the gates, ready to engage the enemy; he clasped his hands together and prayed that those still hurrying towards the castle would find safety to the land in the far south, if the gates had already closed.

As the two armies confronted one another, Bokin knew that he faced a formidable enemy. His own force numbered nearly eighteen hundred men yet the attackers filled all the land in front of him. The second horn blew and the war began. Temujin bowmen notched arrows, sending wave after wave from their sturdy mounts. Flying like a swarm of crazed hornets, they constantly attacked the men on the flanks. Many Helgs fell but more took their place. Only after the last of the arrows had flown did the Temujin leave the field to seek replacements. They were unarmoured and untutored in a mass attack so stood little chance in close quarter combat against the swords of the Helg cavalry.

More of the enemy died in another charge, yet still they pressed forward, two warriors seeming to appear for every one that perished. A counter charge by a company of militia briefly slowed them before the Helgs galloped onwards once more.

Bokin waited, saving his heavy cavalry. He ordered a trot, then a canter. At the last they charged, fighting and cutting a huge wedge into the centre of the Helg line. Some of the Helgs swung their single-bladed scimitars in a reckless fashion and many of their own received a cut from the curved weapons. But many in the attacking force did know how to fight. The sky rang to the sound of death by steel, as blade met blade in an orgy of savagery. The single-bladed scimitars cut one way but the sabres of the Maxilla proved to be more deadly in trained hands. Doubled-edged, they could be thrust and cut into soft flesh underneath swinging arms. In the confined spaces between the horses, the might of the Maxilla men pushed the attackers back. A gap appeared in the centre of the Helg lines. Bokin urged the Maxilla to advance but a horn blew and the Helgs turned away.

Bokin followed but knew he had been tricked. The Helgs had disengaged and now rode directly toward his castle, and in the distance he could see another strong Helg band already a mile ahead. Although he believed that Castle Bokin could never be conquered, the battle had changed. His men would be fighting on the chosen ground of the enemy and the area around the castle would not be particularly conducive for horsemen. That meant a long and tiring battle with sword and spear on foot. With the cottages and store houses adjacent to the castle being full of provisions, a defending army could survive and fight for a considerable time.

The Helgs had clearly planned this as they immediately spread out to encircle Castle Bokin. They had already gained a huge advantage. Lord Bokin considered his adversary. He admired the man for showing an astute understanding of battle tactics yet hated him for attacking his people. He resolved not to underestimate his opponent. Many months of war flashed through his mind. He had known that his initial charge would not hold them, but he had needed time – and now his delaying tactics had failed.

At the end of the first day, when King Leofrick arrived with seven hundred fully-armed soldiers, the attackers still outnumbered them two to one. The cavalry battle had been lost but the war of attrition had begun.

Helg soldiers tried desperately to force entry to the castle over the next three months. The mighty stone fortress had stood unbowed and unbroken for nearly a hundred years; testament to the stonemasons that had built such a worthy castle for the Bokin family.

The twin stone towers, either side of the drawbridge, proudly displayed the scars of previous sieges. The murder holes and archer spaces built into the inner sides of both towers had been used to great effect.

Apart from crossing the moat, the raised drawbridge was the only means of entry. Very difficult to climb, any attempt would result in almost certain death from the secreted bowmen. Even if the drawbridge could be lowered by breaking the chains, a portcullis and inner door of solid oak barred the way. Here burning oil or molten metal could be tipped over the invaders from a hole above.

As the Helgs had found out, the cost to any attacking force was high.

Four huge towers stood in each corner of the square castle, with two more standing either side of the drawbridge. A crenelated parapet with walkways extended all the way round.

Yet the Helgs had tried again and again, even transporting vast quantities of stone and soil to bridge the moat at its narrowest point. But bowmen had rained arrows down on them from the crenellations. Helg archers countered ineffectively, as most of the time they were forced to hide behind wooden shields. Boulders were dropped from the walls onto any warrior carrying a ladder, as well as cauldrons of hot oil before the liquid ran out. The defenders hoped that it would be enough.

On the outer edge of the enemy lines encircling Castle Bokin, Maxilla and the Stormborn used all their might and cunning to keep them occupied: tricks and subterfuge as well as swift attacks. Horsemen probed for any weakness in the lines. Skirmishers attacked with bow and long spear. But any gain would soon be lost. Men perished every day and not only from the constant fighting; infection and disease took their toll as the bodies of the fallen began to stink. Water became a vital commodity for the invaders and, luckily for them, frequent rain helped to quench dry mouths. The damp ground around the castle also helped their cause. It soon churned into a swampy morass making horse movements difficult, and cavalry charges impossible.

Inside Castle Bokin, the stench of death leached into everyone. At first only a few unwary fighters died on the walls, struck by stray arrows, but starvation and sickness took control elsewhere. As the vomiting illness spread, fears grew about the number of soldiers still able to fight. Women carried supplies to the battlements as well as weapons. Some picked up bows and loosed arrows. Children stayed close to the kitchens, taking food to the defenders, but rations thinned. Morale sank lower than a buried corpse. Something had to give.

Lord Bokin had different problems, but luckily water was not one of them. As the Helgs held sway over the local granaries and food stores, his riders had to travel ever-lengthening distances to obtain supplies. Fighting men had voracious appetites. Disease was less of a problem but, even so, every company was ordered to dig trenches well away from any living or fighting areas. With the battleground constantly changing, he found it impossible to keep too many resources in one location, which meant that companies were often situated in the wrong place.

When the first Helgs attacked Renda's home village of Lakeside, he organised the men and countered with a deadly charge. The enemy perished but more began to arrive. Outnumbered, he knew that only death awaited them if they stayed. He led his wife, his grandson, Tarn, and several women into the dense forest. Wynne and four local men soon joined them along with their children and wives. Renda told his wife to lead the women and children south, reminding her to stay well clear of the castle. The men would stay and fight.

Tarn and his neighbours watched and wept from the dense undergrowth, numbed by the brutality of the Helg attack that had swept into their beautiful village. The tranquil setting had been destroyed. Bodies lay where they had fallen, covered in feasting flies and flying insects. Strutting crows and raucous magpies pecked at the bodies, squabbling over the juiciest bits. Trampling soldiers had turned the ground into a disgusting swamp of the dead. The carpenter had been attached to a cartwheel and thrown into the lake, whilst others had been nailed to tall trees. Two young boys screamed in agony as the lash fell on their backs. The posts held firm, but gradually the moaning died on the wind. Some of the women and children had escaped into the woods; a violent end awaited the unlucky ones. No matter the age, all the women were raped, the children forced to watch whilst the men were hacked into small pieces, eagerly devoured by the hungry dogs.

Being too far from the castle, the people of Lakeside had been too slow to flee into the woods. They had been almost wiped out. Ninety-six inhabitants were subsequently found to have been murdered out of a populace of one hundred and twenty-four.

Memories of Wynne being physically restrained by his grandfather solidified in Tarn's mind. Any attack would have proven futile.

Tarn remembered his first fights – the cuts, the bruises, the pain and the constant fear. His bowels had emptied on occasion, pissing down his leg a more frequent occurrence, but Grandfather Renda always stood with him. And Wynne had always watched his back. As his skills improved, so had his boldness, for the Helgs grew lazy. Some had shown little appetite to move on and attack the castle, especially as Lakeside held large supplies of ale and food. Often drunk, they staggered and fell like pigs in a muddy wallow. Wynne would often accompany him on a visit late at night. Stealthily they would creep into Lakeside, cut a few throats and depart like wraiths carrying food or weapons.

Renda began to wonder why the Helgs had changed from a fighting force into a rabble. But the more they deteriorated the more he could kill.

From the security of the woods, their guerrilla attacks intensified as more of the Maxilla clan arrived to take the fight to the enemy.

Renda had constantly requested more men from his lord. Much to his chagrin, his wishes had been denied, but now he could intensify his efforts and take the fight to the enemy. Unfortunately, more Helgs also appeared as if by magic.

Not knowing how tenuous Lord Bokin's hold over the whole battleground was, Renda still pushed for more.

Elsewhere, Lord Bokin and King Leofrick constantly harassed the Helgs surrounding the castle but no breakthrough could be made. Grona, Tarn's father, had led many charges into the enemy lines but all had failed. Bokin ordered him to cease his suicidal attacks as too many good men had fallen to Helg spears.

After three months of fighting in the shadows, the defenders received a boost as fresh Stormborn troops arrived. The extra men tilted the balance. Renda retook the village in a battle lasting two days. Lakeside could be rebuilt but the loss of so many would always haunt them. As the number of dead continued to rise on both sides, Lord Bokin sensed that a small victory could signify the beginning of the end. The battle at Lakeside would subsequently prove him right.

An arrow had creased Tarn's head in the attack and Renda carried a number of cuts, but they pushed on towards Castle Bokin without hesitation, for Helgs still walked on Maxilla lands. Over one hundred men now followed Renda, including two score bowmen, the deadly Temujin having been assigned to his company.

Small groups of sick Helgs tried to fight them as they walked, but they ruthlessly swept aside their feeble attacks. Renda questioned a few of the captives before a swinging axe sealed their fate. Rumours of a shaman worried him. He had met one many years previously and had been lucky. On the other hand, the sickness and diarrhoea of the enemy gave cause for hope.

Renda sensed a golden opportunity on reaching the woods to the east of the castle. The area appeared to hold fewer of the enemy than before. So many Helgs had succumbed to the vomiting illness that others avoided the area. With the Stormborn and the Bokin men harrying the invaders from horseback, the Helgs hidden in the forest had been left relatively untroubled up to now. Even the doughty Prince Wren and his cavalrymen were afraid of hidden archers, but that risk had diminished so it was one worth taking.

Renda immediately attacked the exposed flank. As he moved, a hidden warrior rose from the thick undergrowth and plunged a knife into his neck. An arrow took the attacker in the back as he ran off, but Renda's fate had been sealed.

Tarn cradled him in his arms with his grandfather's blood spurting all over him. He remembered the reek of despair before the rage overcame him. Mind and body surged with energy. Sweat leaked into stained clothes, mixing with the blood of the fallen. With his hands wet and sticky he reached to take his grandfather's broadsword in his clenched fist. As the fury demanded action, Tarn held the sword aloft.

"Charge!"

His men followed, Wynne alongside him. The butchery had begun. Temujin and Maxilla bowmen loosed volley after volley over the heads of their running comrades, before running forward to repeat the process. Men threw down their weapons to beg for mercy. Tarn and his men ignored their pleas. Slash, cut and slice – the blades would do their job as long as strong arms wielded them. Tarn's right arm never faltered as untold power sped through his frame. Fearless of anyone and anything he constantly moved forward. Maxilla warriors followed their mad man, screaming for blood. The drug of battle intoxicating.

So fast did he push forward that soon only the Helg commander and his chosen men stood before him. A blur of steel, a thrust, a flick of the wrist and Tarn's lethal blade brushed across an unsuspecting throat. Blood gushed, men surrendered and like wildfire company after company of Helgs either ran or perished.

Tarn, the crazy unknown, had become a Maxilla hero.

CHAPTER 2

Ten years later

THE LONG SWORD, tarnished with age, hung on the back of the oak door. It served as a reminder of an age gone by when the lands had been ruled by the fear of death. Two smaller blades were mounted on wooden pegs either side of the granite hearth. All had a sad tale to tell.

Tarn sat in his grandfather's chair, cuddling his daughter. The fire gave out more than enough warmth for the whole room and sufficient for the bedchamber. As Lori lay asleep he remembered the bad times, the fearsome battles, the constant empty stomach and the deaths of so many of his kin. Never again would he receive anything from Grandfather Renda, apart from his old sword and easy memories. Perhaps his close resemblance to his Grandfather, and not only in looks, accounted for the fact that he hardly missed his father at all. Grona, son of Renda was a pig. A good fighter but a pig nevertheless. How his mother had kept the peace he would never know, and she had died in childbirth along with his sister, leaving him alone. His father ignored him, as if blaming Tarn for her demise, so little had changed since his birth. Without the love of his Grandfather and

Grandmother Sollos he would have perished at the age of seven. He missed them every day.

Tarn stroked his daughter's dark hair, pulling it back from her eyes so that he could kiss her forehead. The world had once again become a peaceful place – a place where endless days of nothing meant so much. He closed his ice blue eyes and said a prayer to the gods in the heavens. A sigh escaped from his lips. He often wondered whether they ever looked and listened.

Yes, the bad days had gone, but were not forgotten; they were pushed back into the recesses of minds wishing not to remember. So many families had been affected that only the lucky few would not lay flowers on Sacrifice Day. The days had passed slowly at first, as the bodies of the dead had been recovered from fields and woodlands. Grieving families walked around trance-like, unable to comprehend the scale of the slaughter. The wails of mourning filled the air for miles. As month moved into month and season into season, the routine of everyday life returned. At first all needed to tighten their belts but soon new crops grew in the fields. Barley, wheat, potatoes, carrots and turnips all thrived, especially where many had fallen. Given time the land would heal as new growth covered old scars. But the local populace would never recover.

Destroyed homes had been rebuilt using the existing stone and new wood from the nearby forest. Tarn knew nothing about building but he and his brawny friend Wynne soon learnt how to construct a house from a pile of rubble. No single family could survive on its own. Co-operate or starve – the choice was simple, the outcome inevitable. The resulting bonds with neighbours and local villages had enabled a new spirit to rise from the ashes.

Tarn sat comfortably with his sleeping daughter. He enjoyed life, yet often took time to remember the past. In view of the awful memories Wynne often asked him why. The answer had never changed: "I owe it to all the dead."

He recalled the years of recovery. Slowly at first, they had flown by as everyone pitched in to help one another. Even the lazy worked, albeit after a gentle prod from their lord. Out of chaos grew a unified people, demanding change and security. The changes had come from within themselves and the security from Lord Bokin. As the years passed the Maxilla people had continued to recover. Trade from the south and the east flourished, and agreements were signed with the Temujin riders of the north. Through tired eyes Tarn saw himself riding his magnificent stallion once again. A gift from the Temujin was a great honour and Nasan, the leader of the Temujin, had presented it to him personally.

After horse bandits had tried to steal some ponies, Tarn's small Maxilla band had chased and eventually ridden them down. Delivering both the ponies and the thieves had earned Nasan's thanks. Every small act strengthened the bond between the two nations.

He kissed little Lori again, hoping that she would never see the horrors of war in her lifetime.

There was no magnificence in blood, only despair, for splendour came from the land and the sky. Riding the lands had given him a perfect seat from which to see nature at work. The majestic blue high above gave out signals of desire. Combined with the feathery white, they intoxicated him.

His wife, Tasmina, had often travelled with him, searching for a bed of scented wild flowers. Once found, their lovemaking would be frantic, as if seeking each other for the first time. Lori had been conceived on a bed of love, alongside a pool of pure azure. Bathing naked afterwards they had felt their bodies tingle with the cold. They had stepped from the waters holding hands, diving into each other again, their passion running faster than thought. It had been the most memorable moment of Tarn's life, as Tasmina regularly reminded him.

His lovely wife would return shortly and as usual would chide him for his laziness; he preferred to rock his little girl to sleep than to work. A flick of long raven hair, a quick lash of red tongue and a kiss on his cheek would announce her arrival. How could he fall for anyone else when Tasmina loudly announced that she had met her man? What a woman, he thought, as his mind once again wandered back to more pressing matters.

Nearly ten years had passed, and farming flourished in this post-war age. Most families grew more than they required. The fertile soil and the recent years of endless sunshine had helped enormously. Hard work ensured that the harvests found their way to hungry mouths and not left to rot in the fields.

But a new request from the lord had been delivered. Bokin had asked the men folk to attend a meeting to discuss the future sale of crops within the castle grounds. Tarn had agreed in principle, as some thieves had robbed several families at the poorly-organised and undefended market in the woods. Even with this news, Lord Bokin rarely called such a meeting for all the men folk. Tarn guessed that a bigger problem loomed, but no matter what, he felt confident that the Maxilla people would cope.

Such was the easy living that even the talk of distant unrest had failed to worry any of the inhabitants of Lakeside. Good crops gave a plentiful supply of food, local water and strong beer the necessary liquid refreshments, whilst all combined to provide a relatively carefree existence after the hellish war. Lakeside's population needed to forget the past even though the horror still visited the minds of many. A few newcomers had been welcomed. Having lost everything in the battle, Lord Bokin had provided them with the tools for a resettlement programme. There was more than enough land to satisfy the needs of thirty-five people from seven families without upsetting the survivors.

With all his heart, Tarn wished for a quiet and peaceful life for his family and friends; sometimes he even believed it would be possible.

The door crashed open and Wynne made his usual entrance, remembering at the last moment to duck his head under the wooden beam. Long braided hair dangled over his shoulders and a locket hung around his wide neck. Scratching his thick beard and dressed in a soft leather jacket, linen trousers and long boots, he looked like a pirate from the southern oceans that Tarn had once met on his travels. Only the wide-brimmed hat was missing. Tarn tried to imagine Wynne on a ship but no matter how hard he tried the two did not seem compatible.

Wynne ignored the finger on lips and sleeping child.

"Get up. War is coming!"

CHAPTER 3

"Wynne ... shut that bloody door. It's cold out there."

"Right! But you have to listen. I've been at the Bell tavern and there's a lot of talk."

Tarn groaned loudly, then took a deep breath before laying Lori in her small bed.

"There's always talk at The Bell, Wynne. It's a haven for gossip."

"No, this is real. A traveller from the north said so and I believe him."

"Listen Wynne, the travellers always have stories to sell. How much did this one cost?"

"Only one beer ... but that's not the point. His brain is mixed up but he fought in Bokin's Band."

"What?"

"I've never heard of him before but he called himself Folmar Metton," Wynne said.

I have, but that was years ago, I believed he had resigned his commission, Tarn thought.

"Are you sure he said Bokin's Band, Wynne? Because, if it's the same man, he retired some time ago."

"Yes, Bokin's Band. His mind wandered but he mentioned soldiers and magic. He is convincing," Wynne said.

"Forget it," Tarn said without much conviction. He turned away, but his mind dwelled on thoughts of horror and destruction. The exploits of Bokin's Band were the stuff of legends, and he should know, having been a member for some time. They never ran, they never surrendered and they rarely lost. If this man had spoken the truth then maybe ... but why had he run or even deserted? Tarn looked at Wynne; he could drink anyone under a table. With his mind in turmoil Tarn wanted to dismiss any notion of war out of hand. Yet the more he thought, images of foul deeds swirled around inside his head.

Wynne ignored Tarn. The big man lowered his bulk into the matching chair on the other side of the hearth, but not before picking up Tarn's pewter tankard and downing the contents in one go. Wiping his huge hand across his face, he belched, farted and peered into the dancing flames, oblivious to his friend's frown.

Tarn looked at his friend and longed, not for the first time, for his simplistic outlook on life. Wynne liked to sit and think, especially over a large meal accompanied by good ale or mead. Over the years some folk had mistaken his casual attitude for stupidity and had tried to take advantage. It would always end badly for them – usually with a dunking in a convenient water butt. Never one to hold a grudge for too long, the big man would haul them out of their watery resting hole before pushing a tankard of frothy ale into their shaking hands. Wynne had few enemies and many friends. He had been friends with Tarn since childhood and as opposites attract they were closer than many kin. Tarn understood better than anyone the sorrow that lay buried deep within Wynne's broken heart.

As Tarn tried to take in his friend's tale he sensed that their chalk and cheese partnership may once again be needed. Too many questions needed answers and none would be found sitting inside his house.

"Move your arse, big man – time to go."

As if by magic, Tasmina appeared through the back door. She wore a long dress of emerald green and her long hair flowed freely. Tarn thought that she looked like a goddess. She ran both hands through her hair and paused to take in the scene before placing slender hands on her hips. Tarn left the comfort of his chair and embraced her before she could speak, then placed Lori into her open arms. It was only after kissing her generous and responsive lips that he casually mentioned his need to depart immediately.

"How very convenient, husband. Maybe I won't be here when you return?" She held the front door open but gave him a hard kick up the backside as he passed. Wynne offered a weak smile, a smile that instantly vanished on seeing the wrath of the raven-haired angel.

"Tarn. Where are we going?"

"Castle Bokin. The Lord will know more than we do. Your tale is worrying, but I pray that you are wrong, you big lump." Hitting Wynne on the back always made his hand sting but he would never admit it.

"Good. The Castle tavern serves excellent mead." The returning slap almost knocked Tarn over. "Sorry Captain." After all these years Wynne occasionally called him by his rank. Tarn had hoped that his friend would have stopped by now as the title always brought back the wrong memories, but it was not to be.

After a thirty-minute walk the two companions stood before the open drawbridge of Castle Bokin.

Flowering water lilies floated on the moat as ducklings followed their parents across the calm waters. Rushes and sedges grew on the fringes. Trout rose to take flies and insects from the water. The backdrop of ugly slate-grey stone, weathered by wind and rain, looked incongruous against nature's tranquillity.

Unlike most moats, the one around Castle Bokin was not a cesspit. The lord had learnt about the effects of human waste after the siege, and had taken preventative steps to avoid a repetition. On pain of imprisonment, no one was allowed to dump their excreta into the lake. It resulted in a trade for shit-shovellers. They could be seen on a daily basis transporting barrels of liquid to a nearby quarry. If the wind blew from the north, the smell would be overpowering but it appeared to keep the wolves and bears away.

Scarred like a granite cliff, the castle proudly displayed the weathering of age. It had served as a refuge, a meeting place and as a symbol of might against any attacking force. The Maxilla clan had stubbornly defended their lands when necessary, due, in no small part, to the fortress that served as a rallying point.

The free folk of the hills, the Stormborn, the riders of the plains, the Temujin, and even a few of the elusive Woodmen had come to the aid of the Maxilla people in the past. United in friendship, they had fought and died together. The pain of so many deaths had washed over families like a flood of endless tears. Even so many years after the Helgs fled back to their mountain retreats, the anguish of one family or another could be heard on windless nights. It would take even longer for the nightmares to ebb away into the shadows of the past. Life had improved considerably since then but the dead would never return.

Looking at the castle always brought the memories flooding back. At the age of nineteen Tarn thought himself a man; at the victory celebrations, eight months later, he knew he had been wrong. He had been a frightened boy who somehow survived the months of carnage to lead a charge that finally broke the Helgs' ranks and all but crushed them.

He remembered the snarling face of his father as Lord Bokin presented him with gold coins to rebuild his grandfather's home, and a large plot of land of his own. His father had recklessly charged into battle many times, and failed many times, causing the demise of too many men – a brave man but a pig-headed one. A father that loathed his son even more after watching his initial coolness in battle turn into a suicidal charge and to win where he had failed. That leadership had ultimately turned potential defeat into victory, the victory that Grona had craved for himself. They had barely spoken since.

Tarn and Wynne strode across the drawbridge and under the iron portcullis before entering the outer bailey. The doorway to the dungeons led off to the left alongside the barracks. On the other side of the bailey the blacksmith's hammer sang. Horses stood patiently, waiting to be groomed or fed. They could almost taste fresh bread as the smell drifted on the breeze from the adjacent kitchens. Men had already gathered alongside the deep well as the overflowing Castle tavern rang to the dull ring of pewter tankards, and noisy chatter. Ahead lay the gate to the inner bailey, Lord Bokin's dwellings and the shrine to the gods.

Surprisingly busy with common folk and soldiers, they sensed a storm brewing even though the sun shone. As they walked towards a small platform the voices dissipated. A man spat in front of them.

"Come to save us again ... boy." Grona's insult echoed off the stone walls. Although the taunt still bit, Tarn ignored it. He had closed his mind to the insults over the years and looked straight ahead.

"That's Captain to you, dog breath." Wynne said.

"That rank ceased years ago," Grona sneered.

"Don't push me ... *Father* Grona," Wynne said.

Tarn knew that Wynne cared little for Grona's feelings. His sarcasm bit deeply. He relished seeing such rage on the face of a man that had never recognised his only son, let alone be around to care for him.

Lord Bokin made a timely entrance as the temperature rose. Dressed in a tunic of dark blue with a surcoat of black, he cast a drab picture against the bright sun directly above. Even the Bokin insignia of the 'Leaping Hare' appeared faded.

"I summoned you here to discuss robbers in our woods. That is no longer of major importance for other matters demand our attention. Some of you have heard stories as rumours travel fast. Regrettably in this case, many are likely to be true. I wanted to be sure of the facts before summoning you, but as so many are here you need to know what I believe is the truth."

As Lord Bokin addressed the crowd, Tarn saw concern mixed with puzzlement on the faces of those assembled. Bokin had their full attention now.

"It is feared that the Helgs have risen again for it is said that old wounds have been opened and old scores are to be settled." His dark brown eyes set deep into a troubled face had lost all sparkle.

The men looked at each other. Angry faces vied with those showing disbelief. Another war loomed on the horizon. As Lord Bokin watched the men, some stood still, whilst others raised fists and screamed obscenities. Many groaned loudly. A serving girl dropped her tray of mugs, the ale falling on those nearest. Another woman failed to stifle a scream. The blacksmith's hammer fell from lifeless hands.

"No! Not Again!" Men shouted with rage and despair, confused in a fog of uncertainty.

"Then we march ... *now*," Grona demanded, raising his fists in the air towards his supporters.

"No! We do not." Lord Bokin waved his arms in the air, demanding quiet. "Listen to me. We send out scouts, we prepare. Then we fight."

"My Lord Bokin ... with respect, delays cost lives. Hit them hard and hit them now."

Several voices echoed his words. Others shouted in opposition. Insults echoed within the enclosed space.

"Enough! I am your lord. You are an officer, a Captain in my band, and you will do as I bid, Grona." Bokin's face turned scarlet. He breathed long and hard.

Tarn knew Grona well; the older man understood the signs. He would play the game but on his terms.

"As you wish ... my Lord," he said contemptuously. Held firmly at his sides, two clenched fists turned white.

Lord Bokin ignored him. "And what do you have to say, Captain Tarn?" The strong voice reverberated around the courtyard.

Heads turned in Tarn's direction. Eyes bored into him from all sides. Tarn felt like a piece of metal between the hammer and the anvil. A restored commission in the army was the last thing he suspected today.

"Lord, if true, this is a grievous blow to our peace. Is it really as you say?"

He heard his father toss an insult his way before Lord Bokin could answer.

"I regret that this is likely to be true. Folmar Metton, the man that told his tale to all who would listen in The Bell tavern, is a loyal member of my band. He has been patrolling the edge of the northern lands for some years; a thankless task but one in which he excelled. He was captured by the Helgs and tortured to the edge of insanity, but managed to escape with his mind in tatters. We will honour him later, but for now, you will listen to his story."

Two members of the Castle guard supported a man as he shuffled forward. The lines on his face looked like deep cart tracks in mud; his eyes gloomy like dusk. Brushing aside the men, he tried to stand tall.

"I have been away for too long … my eyesight is poor, but with help … my memory has returned. The Helgs want revenge. They are gathering together, practising their battle skills. I fear the … the eyes like the mists of time."

He screamed like a wounded animal as his hands covered a ravaged face.

"You must listen. My mind was lost to me once, I travelled, wandered aimlessly but I hung onto the vision of this castle. It is my home, please … listen. War is coming … the pain … no … leave my head."

Without the support of the soldiers Folmar Metton would have fallen into the dust. He shouted as the warriors led him away. "You must prepare, they are vindictive and without mercy."

Lord Bokin's shoulders sagged as he chose his next words.

"Our enemies appear to have regrouped, rearmed and are nearly ready to invade once more. However there is something or someone behind the Helgs. Folmar repeated the words – the Horned Demon – the Horned Demon ..."

His words trailed away and all present strained to hear more.

Questions raced from man to man, yet none had any answers: "What is this demon? Where does it come from? When? Why?"

"So now you know. I repeat my question, Captain. What do you say?"

"We need more information, Lord, as we must not underestimate their strength. Riders need to be sent as soon as possible. If this is war, we must prepare and take all precautions." The thought of being caught unaware again pained Tarn's head. And although he spoke with some certainty, the contents of his stomach threatened to rise in his throat.

"Good! Then you and Wynne will ride north tomorrow, together with a full company of Bokin's Band. Gather the information. Bring it back at all costs. You have sixteen, maybe seventeen days."

Grona butted in. "Enough! You give this quest to a lucky ... pup. Let me go in his stead, Lord. I have earned the right."

"You will treat me with respect!"

Grona declined his head.

"For your bravery, Grona, you have earned the right. But the animosity between father and son is well known. You are rash; Tarn is dispassionate. Why should I jeopardise the mission?"

"Because I am the only one who has ever been near this Horned Demon and lived to tell the tale." Grona stood tall, pushing his chest out, revelling in his own self-importance.

Gasps escaped unbelieving lips. Noise levels grew as the crowd moved closer.

"Quiet!" Lord Bokin shouted. "Now, tell me more Grona."

"Lord Bokin, now is not the time to relive old hurts. Believe me - I have knowledge that could be valuable. You also need my sword. I do not have any scars on my back." The casual insult drew angry shouts.

Grona didn't stop. He must have felt that he had to say more to satisfy Lord Bokin. "At the last battle I saw a Horned Demon some distance away and, luckily, I survived. It appeared and then it was gone. There is nothing else to say."

When clad as normal in a black leather jerkin and soft woollen breeches, strangers would have taken Grona for any other rich man - as he was. But today, in fighting garb of jerkin over tunic and with a large sword strapped to his back, he looked a very different beast. Two daggers and a small axe on his belt added to the effect. Grona liked to be ready.

A fierce determination burned in Grona's heart. With his lack of fear he would fight until he dropped. He never turned his back on a fight. On this mission he would be a valuable asset. He had also seen the Horned Demon, but could he be trusted?

"Why did no other warrior mention this, Grona?" Lord Bokin said.

"It was a mere moment, enough for me - but for others, who can say?"

Lord Bokin rubbed a hand over his chin as lips closed over grinding teeth.

"I have never doubted your bravery or your aggression. It is such a pity that you cannot preserve it for the battlefield. Already you have questioned my leadership several times; one more and you will be shackled for a week. Do I make myself clear?"

The snarl disappeared, leaving Grona shocked in its wake. "Yes, my Lord."

"Good. I still have my doubts but this mission is more important than family quarrels. Do I have your word on this?"

Reluctantly, the words flowed from pursed lips." You have my word."

"Then I order you to follow your son, for he has earned the right to lead. As … I commanded."

With fingers running through his thick grey beard, and eyes afire with menace, Grona hesitated once more. He looked at his lord, then at Tarn.

"So be it." He gripped his sword ever tighter as his heart pumped more venom around his frame. His followers moved in, protecting their leader. All eyes turned to Grona.

Wynne's right hand opened the front of his jerkin and freed the hilt of his sword. Bile once again rose in Tarn's mouth as he stared at the vengeful face of his father. Tarn knew that no matter what he did, Grona's hatred for him would never cease.

Words of warning came to mind as images of stupid charges led by a crazed man assailed him. It was his company, not Grona's, and it would have more chance of success without his sire's interference.

Pressing his way through the crowd to speak to Lord Bokin proved difficult. Hands clapped him on the back as he passed. Some warriors wanted to talk, others to gather round and show their support. Swords and armour clanked wherever he turned. Lord Bokin had departed by the time he reached the entrance to the inner bailey, and the guards made it known that their master was not to be disturbed.

Unenthusiastically, he left to prepare for the long ride.

~~~

Sitting in a chair staring at a cold wall was anything but normal, Tasmina considered. But she would leave her husband to his thoughts as she recalled some of her own.

From the day she first noticed boys, Tarn turned her head and her heart as it raced away with desire. Such feelings had come as a big shock, but he had such an easy manner, being polite with young and old alike and assisting wherever he could, that she could not stop herself. He cared for people. Tasmina guessed that was due to the love and influence of his grandparents.

His willingness to try anything amazed her. Be it a tree to be climbed, races to be run, apples to scrump, or even a hot pie that needed rescuing from a window ledge, Tarn would be first in line. His fighting skills, unimpressive at first, improved marginally but he lost more than he won. He wasn't one to hold a grudge, and with big Wynne as his closest companion his popularity soared.

Tasmina fondly remembered their first kiss. Tarn had taken an interest in another young girl so she had to act fast. She made an announcement when he was absent on a hunting trip. On his return a bemused Tarn received a blessing from everyone he met. Tasmina kissed him passionately in front of the whole village, his grandparents gave their approval and he was hooked. She often chided him for his lack of words at the time, but smiled when he retorted that he knew how lambs felt living close to a she-wolf.

They married when she reached the lawful age of sixteen. Living in the same house with Grandfather Renda and Grandmother Sollos cemented the bond with extra love. Those two wonderful people had showered her with as much affection as her own parents. Contented with her lot, she had planned for their perfect future together. She reminisced over her dreams that the happy times would last forever.

But then the Helgs marched south and her carefree world turned into a slaughterhouse.

Tasmina had been lucky. She had travelled south with her parents to the coastal town of Pelton, as her mother's relatives had organised a gathering to celebrate a new born baby. Tarn could not be excused from his duties so remained at home, learning new skills under his lord's tutelage.

When news of the Helgs reached them, she had worried over his safety. He believed that the gods had favoured her. Tarn told her later that if she had remained she would now be resting under a pile of earth.

The loss of Renda and Sollos within a few months left them both disconsolate. For a long and empty time, they hardly communicated with each other, both lost in protective bubbles, afraid that they would burst at any time. As they discussed later, talking would only have resurrected the memories and the pain. But when the dam burst, the waters washed away the hurt of the body and cleansed the soul.

Busy with the rebuilding of Renda's house, as well as others in Lakeside, they found the days tiring. Each new dawn appeared to greet them a little sooner than the last. All attempts to conceive eluded them as year after year flew past quicker than they could imagine. Tarn was promoted to Captain in the Bokin Band and travelled far and wide in the service of the Maxilla people. Tasmina could not remember a time when he complained. Her love grew with his dedication to his people, yet they both wanted more. As the real power in their marriage she understood what her husband yearned for. The travelling, the potions, the secrecy - Tarn never knew how difficult it was to conceive their child and she had vowed that he never would.

Tarn had asked Lord Bokin if he could resign his commission once Lori had been safely born. In view of the new peace, he concurred, but only on the understanding that Tarn could be recalled at any time.

It had worked well. The family had grown together, and the old love became new love. Tarn changed. He relaxed with Tasmina and he always unwound when he enjoyed a night at the Castle tavern with Wynne. He had grown his fair hair long, in keeping with the modern style, and secured it with a silver clasp at the neck. But Tasmina refused any request for him to grow a beard as his previous attempts had ended in a mass of fluffy wool. No more night-time adventures with a face like a sheep, she had scolded. A rich smile lit her face as she remembered the chase of the sharp knife and hot water around the house.

But today … today would be remembered as an evil day.

The past had returned to haunt the families of Lakeside once again. When Tarn told her the news she had sobbed in his arms until no more tears could fall. With her breast heaving so much, a strong pain surged into her torso which forced her to lie down. Lying on their bed gave her the relief that she sought yet the pain refused to abate entirely. Tarn had tried to comfort her, vowing not to take any stupid chances. But Tasmina refused to listen. She cursed him for making empty promises as she tried to contemplate the awful possibility of life without her man.

When she found her senses returning to normal, the pragmatic side of her brain slowly began to take over. She scolded herself for being weak and selfish. Tarn had to go to war to defend all of his people, which was more important than her feelings. He had no choice and neither did she; Tasmina knew that she had to be strong for all three of them. She would stand tall and proud when he left, and afterwards she would wait and cope.

Lori had only seen two summers but already she controlled her father. After Tarn had delivered the bad news, Tasmina used her intuition and sat Lori on his lap. His face instantly changed as she demanded attention, the smile a joy to see. It had worked, for a few precious hours anyway.

After they placed Lori in her small bed and the daylight faded into night, Tasmina confronted her husband. "You have sat all afternoon, staring into space. I know the shattering of peace ails you, but … I sense there is more. Enough! What is it?"

Tasmina still felt her husband's heart pounding away as she held his hand. He smiled half-heartedly as she squeezed a little harder. "I am sorry, my beloved. You know me too well. I will not even try to lie to you. If the reports are true then a terrible history will repeat itself all over again. Many will die but I have other fears. My father is riding with us. Bokin gave me charge of the mission, but by making the declaration public he slapped Grona down. I saw the rage burning like hot coals. There is no doubt in my mind that I will face two enemies. I will tackle anyone man to man but the devious foe can be lethal, especially if he purports to be with you. Who knows whether I can trust my own father?"

"So, husband of mine, your aging father rears his ugly head once more. Tell me what happened." Tarn left nothing out. When he had finished, Tasmina said, "He is clever, sometimes too clever for his own good. But remember this, Tarn, you are in command. If he disobeys your orders ..."

"I know, but he is still my flesh and blood."

"The kin that disowned you and ignored you ever since, that is unless you wish to consider the abuse and casual insults on the few occasions when your paths have crossed. No wonder he hates being called 'Father Grona.' That insult must really hurt as he made no attempt to be a father to you. And has he ever seen his granddaughter?" Tasmina's voice rose in pitch as she raised her head higher in the air. "Grona is a swine, he always will be. You have ignored the problem for too long Tarn. Soon the moment will come and you must confront it. With the prospect of another war looming it is not the perfect time; nevertheless you must act swiftly and decisively if there are any challenges to your leadership."

Tasmina had wandered around the room as she spoke. She stopped before her man and raised his chin with her right hand. "You only hesitate because this animosity is between you and your own kin. Rightly you have feelings for Grona, for whatever he has become, he still sired you. However in our hour of need there is no place for personal sentiments. You are my strong and loving husband. I know that you will make the right choices in dealing with your father as and when necessary." She bent down and kissed him passionately.

Tarn stood up to embrace his little firebrand. "There is so much truth in what you say my love. As usual your eyes see clearly through the mist of my trepidation. I will deal with it in my own way. Kin or no kin, he will listen and obey."

Tasmina beamed. "I love you more than I could ever believe possible."

"And I you, for love fears no dangers."

"My beautiful man. Now take me to bed and I'll show you what you'll be missing on your long ride."

~~~

Before the rising sun could show its face, the smell of freshly oiled leather filled the outer bailey as twenty two armed men saddled up ready to depart.

Sheepskin pelts covered the horses' backs. They would also double up as blankets for the men once in the hills. The mounted men rubbed their hands together, cold despite their jerkins and leggings. Both horses and warriors left vapour trails as they exhaled. They sat impatiently awaiting the order to depart. A single warrior sat on a huge grey mare, alone by the inner gate, determined to lead the company out of the castle no matter the Lord's command. Tarn knew the signs; Grona was making a point.

Lord Bokin and several officers had risen early.

"For the last two days, I have spent my waking hours thinking of ways to protect our people. All that can be done is already in place or being prepared. Many riders have already left with messages to our allies, for we need assistance and news. If the Helgs have truly risen against us, then my vision of peace has collapsed, but we will not be found wanting, nor will we be taken by surprise. I give you my solemn oath that your families will be protected inside these walls. We are Maxilla and we stand together, no matter what."

The men murmured their thanks as Lord Bokin reached up to shake Tarn's hand.

"Good luck and may the gods be with you," he said.

Tarn gave the order from the back of his warhorse. Whatever his personal problems, the company had to succeed. Failure could not be considered for the lives of too many innocents depended on them. His thoughts turned to Tasmina, Lori and the promise that he had made as he rode under the portcullis.

Apart from the lord and his men, only the squires saw their departure, yet all those safely abed would soon wonder how many would return.

CHAPTER 4

AFTER SHE HAD said her farewells to her husband, Tasmina wept. When the tears stopped she visited her two friends, not only for joint comfort, but to outline her plans.

Visits to the blacksmith, the carpenter and to Castle Bokin swiftly followed. Tasmina refused to consider any objections. She laid out her ideas, and told them what she wanted. Eventually … all agreed to assist. Tasmina and friends were going to train the women and youngsters. They would learn how to use a hunting bow or wield a dagger in anger. Those already proficient could help to train others.

Her meeting with Lord Bokin proved the most fruitful. Tasmina hit him like a fireball, her words of passion ringing off the castle walls. Undeterred by his few objections she battered away until he agreed. Now all they needed was a workable plan.

With so many men already preparing to leave, they were resolute that Castle Bokin and the surrounding lands of the Maxilla would not be caught wanting in the event of an attack.

Lord Bokin spent many hours with the commander of the garrison and Tasmina. His riders would patrol up to five miles from the castle, leaving the inner ring to the men of the garrison and Tasmina's group. Bokin was delighted. Not only would the lands adjacent to the castle be protected from an unlikely source, but due to their careful preparations, he could spend less time worrying about a surprise attack behind him.

Many people from the surrounding districts answered the call. They were frightened but determined not to let their men folk down. The Maxilla clan grew ever closer.

Tasmina's anger drove her. How dare these soldiers take her man away? How dare they threaten her daughter? She felt great pride in seeing so many of her friends and neighbours coming together to resist the enemy. If Helg soldiers arrived, she was determined that a volley of arrows awaited them.

CHAPTER 5

THE BEGINNING OF their ride would normally be considered easy, as the company rode over fertile plains and onto gently rolling hills. But this was no normal ride. Small talk soon evaporated as each man remembered the past. Old fears and visions grew in their minds. The plodding horses kept up a good pace, every stride taking the company nearer to their destiny. Only the complaints of the saddle-sore broke the silence.

The sun had risen over a sky of blue with soft clouds in attendance. The men and horses began to freely perspire. Metal clanked on metal. Leather hardened in the heat. Sweaty hands controlled the reins. Thoughts of home fought with concerns over the unknown as each man tried to concentrate on the task ahead.

Heading west, they had planned to meet up with Stormborn cavalry once they entered their lands. Many friendships would be reunited but not in the manner that they would wish.

They could see the towering white-topped mountains at the top of the world. Some warriors made a sign of homage to the gods, others prayed. Most asked for protection. A further three days' ride would find them at the bottom of the hills, yet

Tarn had riders covering the flanks in case of any unexpected attacks. The nearer they got the more their thoughts hardened to the job in hand.

Grona had continued to lead with his trusty band of four but the remaining men considered him no more than a scout. Thus his attempts to undermine his only son failed. He contented himself with insults, which also failed to have any effect.

Tarn called a halt in the middle of a small copse at the end of the first day's riding. Sheltered from wind and rain, the camp provided a refuge for both man and horse. Spirits rose as hot food dropped into empty stomachs. A joker swore that his stomach rang like a bell as the food fell. Grona sat apart with his small band; all attempts to invite others to his private faction had failed.

The night passed slowly, yet tired eyes gave way to sleep ... eventually.

Two more tiring days of riding passed. Apart from some farmers and their families, they saw no signs of any of their allies or, more importantly, of their enemies. The farmers pushed baskets of food into their hands. Tarn returned the favour by telling them of the dangers, advising them to leave and seek the security of Castle Bokin or to travel south to Harbourside. Despite his entreaties he doubted that many would listen.

On the third night they made camp under a covering of beech and oak. A brook babbling around a trio of the large trees provided fresh water. Set in a slight hollow, the leafy ground would provide shelter from a strong wind that had blown in from the east. The horses tethered near a spread of bushes would also benefit. As they were close to the Helg border, Tarn posted a heavier than normal watch. He ordered that, even though the company was nearing exhaustion, every man would tend to their weary mounts before they sank into their blankets. Dog-tired, the men complied before gratefully embracing their beds yet all slept fitfully.

A call to arms woke the sleeping band an hour before dawn. Swords rapidly found their way into familiar hands as the company spread out like a living fan.

A host of riders emerged out of the morning mist, their horses moving slowly. Tarn's men stood in silence, ready to defend themselves. No one moved.

"Bokin Band, we come in peace. The Stormborn bring news."

A sigh of relief swept the camp as a well-armed troop of over fifty men rode in, flying the Black Hawk flag of the Stormborn. Dressed in green tunics, brown leggings and trousers they would be hard to see in the woods. Behind them came the Temujin, the taciturn men of the plains, leading a number of fresh horses. Compared to the Stormborn they looked like a bunch of undisciplined ragamuffins with their betters. But the variety of clothing, headgear and poor manners disguised a band of efficient killers.

A rangy man dismounted from his horse, moving with the agility of an acrobat. His long flowing hair gave grace to his fluid movements, as did the soft suede jacket hanging from wide shoulders.

"Welcome, my brothers in arms, and to you, Tarn. It has been too long since we last met. My commiserations – I see you are still only a Captain," he said with a grin. "For those who do not know me, I am Wren, the son of King Leofrick."

"Welcome indeed my brother, or should I say Prince – it is good to see you after all this time," Tarn said as he took the offered hand in his own. "And by the way, you still owe me a full silver after the bet we made."

"Would that be in the tavern at Harbourside?"

"No. It would be on the boat at Harbourside before I threw you into the water. If I recall correctly the bet was that you could swim."

"Sorry, err ... stupid of me. But you know the feeling when the ale is that good," the Prince said.

Those listening hooted, shouting for more of the story as a silver coin exchanged hands.

"That's enough," Tarn said. "Prince Wren is welcome here ... now that he has paid his debt." The men laughed even louder, lightening the earlier mood.

"Call me Wren, as before. I do not come to lead. Remember, I have seen you fight."

"And I you."

A loud cheer went up. Many soldiers remembered Prince Wren's valour from the war.

King Leofrick had led the initial Stormborn forces towards the Maxilla lands, ordering his son to remain at Castle Stoke. The Prince had not been idle in his duties. Daily excursions into his northern lands had revealed nothing. He pushed further north into the lower hills of the Helg domain with the same result. After many weeks of searching he ceased his patrols. It was clear that the enemy had thrown all their resources into the strike at Castle Bokin. Disobeying his father, he led half the remaining cavalry – some three hundred men – east towards the lands of the Maxilla clan. The rest would protect the realm in his absence.

Prince Wren seldom gambled, but in this case he believed that the end result justified the means. The Helgs had to be beaten.

The stench of war greeted his arrival at the ever-changing battle lines, some three months into the campaign. His head ached like an unwanted hangover, only far worse. Animals lay rotting where they had fallen. Smoke billowed across the fields. Decomposing bodies lay everywhere, although a few soldiers were trying to burn as many corpses as they could.

They shuffled along the endless road of the dead with rags wrapped tightly around their faces. Prince Wren sympathised with them.

The King was furious. His son had disobeyed him. Leaving the homelands at the mercy of robbers and attacks from outsiders could be deemed a treasonable offence. The two argued long and hard. Lord Bokin acted as an intermediary and, after a cooling of tempers, an uneasy truce prevailed. Arguing that fresh troops would be a huge advantage, Bokin persuaded the king to delay judgement until after the final battle.

Prince Wren's cavalry were assigned to the south-eastern sector, well away from his father and his men. As he passed through the lines, Grona poured scorn on him for his late arrival. Jeers and taunts from two sets of allies did nothing to lighten the atmosphere.

However it soon became apparent that the fresh cavalry troops, eager and ready to fight, lifted the spirits of the morose men they joined.

They laid down a marker to the enemy in their first battle. Prince Wren's battalion would not take a step backwards. Sullen soldiers, worn down by a drain and ditch mentality, received a boost. What they gained they held. Little by very little the tide began to turn, slowly squeezing the attackers between a ring of steel and a granite fortress.

An immediate bond of friendship formed between Prince Wren and Tarn when they first met. As the two discussed the details of the war, a mutual respect and admiration grew. Wren marvelled at Tarn's guerrilla tactics and Tarn admired the Prince's skills on horseback. They began to work together as a team, foot soldiers and horsemen with one goal – to kill the enemy.

After the last battle the two had drunk themselves into a stupor. Wynne had carried them to the nearest barn and thrown them onto the hay before re-joining those that could take their ale.

It had taken over five years for their paths to cross again, but since that day at Harbourside the two had frequently ridden into the northern lands, as well as their own.

He was a couple of years older than Tarn, but Prince Wren's looks belied a thirty-one-year-old frame.

His kin believed that his wanderings would cease when he married the beautiful Adeline from the southern lands, especially as she had provided three sons and a daughter – heirs all to the Stormborn throne. Whilst he doted on them, his heart soared like an eagle whenever he rode the lands of his forbears. Always fair, always first, his people adored him, even though he forbade them from using his nickname, little bird.

"Late again ... Prince. As usual, the Stormborn are slow to join the fight these days, that's if you have the guts for one."

"It's so good to see you too, *Father* Grona. Maybe you can show us how to hold a sword and wield an axe. Small ones, of course," he said mischievously.

A ripple of laughter followed. Grona crossed his arms at the warrior's insult, glaring malevolently at Wren.

"Still humourless, are we *Father*?"

Tarn quickly stepped between them.

"It really is good to see you again, Wren. Where have all the months gone? Alas I see a wrinkle or two on your brow but then you are much older than I." He chuckled, but a frown crossed his face. "What news do you bring?"

"The news is strange indeed but firstly my apologies. We have been delayed but not idle. Lord Bokin sent out riders to all his allies as soon as Folmar Metton's story was revealed. He tasked us to warn our folk closest to the Helg lands and move them to safety. The Temujin have supplied many horses for this purpose and, as you have seen, Nasan's men have joined us with extra mounts. An evacuation is in full swing, yet some will not leave their lands."

"I also have seen that stubbornness," Tarn said. All the men knew that if the Helgs attacked, those staying in the outlying hamlets and farms would not live long.

"Have you seen any Helgs, little bird?" Wynne said.

"Never interrupt a man in full flow. I am getting there, big man." Wren chuckled.

"Then get on with it," Wynne replied, trying to be serious.

As the laughter died, Wren's face hardened.

"Naturally, we sent out scouts." His head turned towards the moving figure of Grona. "They came across a few Helg camps, as I and my company did, all manned by young men and boys. None over the age of twenty and all poorly equipped for battle. They fought bravely but readily surrendered when ordered to do so."

"They were not Helgs then." Grona spat out the words. "Are you sure they were not little girlies?"

Wren's hand moved to the hilt of his sword as Grona stood ready, a savage gleam in his eyes.

Tarn savagely back handed the old man's face. His cold blade at Grona's throat prevented any response.

"Father! Enough! You have spat at me, abused me and tried your hardest to undermine me. Now you insult our allies. If you wish to continue, you will behave like a normal soldier under my command. If not, leave now – but I warn you that if you ever abuse me or my friends again, I will cut your stomach wide open."

Grona could see the hatred seeping from every pore of Tarn's body.

He looked into his son's cloudy eyes and saw a berserker warrior. He knew that one false move could end his life in an instant and he would be powerless to stop it. Now he realised how his son had led the troops into battle all those years ago and had won against all the odds. A berserk warrior did not understand fear or death. A little pride ran through his body, but it soon dissipated as the tip of the dagger drew a trickle of blood.

Grona bit his tongue. He knew that he could not return to his lord for his name would forever be tainted and he, judged disloyal or even worse as a coward.

"I will defer to your wishes."

With shoulders hunched and head lowered, he turned away.

Tarn knew that he had won.

"You will stay and listen along with the rest of the company. When we depart, you will be lead scout."

Tarn saw the look of surprise on Grona's weathered face as he trudged back to his place in the ranks. But his eyes still burned with defiance.

All eyes turned back to Wren – the prince who had charged the Helg lines time and again all those years ago. A prince that still rode frequently with his men, for to him, patrolling the Stormborn lands made him feel more alive than sitting in a draughty castle ever could. Those that knew him listened with respect.

"Yes ... well, I'll continue. All the time we spent in the villages seemed unreal, false if you like, as if parts of the structures did not exist. Gossamer-thin, they wavered like a spider's web in the wind. We wondered whether our sight had deceived us, yet the buildings were solid enough when we touched them. The young men fought well around the Horned Demon."

"What demon, little bird?" Wynne said.

"We saw paintings of a huge demon, horned and full of fire in several places. Here the fighters threw everything at us, as if possessed. I believe that something or someone exerted a control over them, yet our searches yielded nothing."

"Folmar Metton. The message?" Wynne asked.

"Who knows?" Wren said. "There are so many gaps, so much that we do not understand. But someone is leading them, of that I am sure."

"They have ... a shaman," Grona said reluctantly.

With all eyes now directed at him, Grona hesitated, looked at Tarn, saw the nod and continued.

"I have met him briefly once before. At the beginning of the last battle all those years ago, some of the Helgs fought manically, their strength unbelievable, almost inhuman. A deep cut from a broadsword would normally send any warrior to the land of the true gods but some carried on fighting regardless. Shortly thereafter they would suddenly fall to the ground, even if no man stood near. As I watched, a shaman appeared at the far edge of the battlefield, too far away to reach. He quickly vanished like a wraith in the night. I questioned a few captives after the battle. They said that a shaman, Myracadonis, arrived some years before the war. His preaching had converted some young boys into a small but fanatical army. Personally selected by Myracadonis, they felt little pain due to an evil brew that they took on a daily basis."

"Why has this never been mentioned before?"

"The war had ended. No sign of the shaman could be found. We all celebrated, wishing to wash the stains from our bodies and the horrors from our hearts." Grona had stated the obvious. When the war ended, everyone wanted to forget and allow time to heal the hurt.

Tarn stroked his hair. "How can you be sure that the Helgs have a shaman? Your words to Lord Bokin mentioned a Horned Demon, nothing else – or am I confused?"

"I told Lord Bokin that I survived the Horned Demon. I lied."

Men jeered, some shouted traitor. Anger rose throughout the ranks. Tarn raised his hands for silence. "Why did you lie?"

"You need me, one way or another. You think I would miss a fight by hiding behind a castle wall."

"And the shaman, did he exist or is this another lie?" Tarn growled.

"My eyes did not deceive me. He stood on the fringe of the battlefield and ... I do not lie."

"You expect us to believe you when your own words have condemned you? But enough; our Lord will deal with your lies when we return ..."

"If we return," Grona said.

"I intend to return, even if you have doubts."

"You have questioned and thus I will answer. I only have doubts over your leadership." Like a baying mob, those in Tarn's company closest to Grona swung towards him. His band of four drew their swords whilst Grona looked straight into his son's face.

"Stand down," Tarn ordered. "All of you stand down now."

Men on both sides sheathed their swords as the voice of command rang out. Tarn sensed that any wrong word now would be quickly followed by bloodshed.

"Even so. I lead and you do not. No more lying Grona. Convince me that I can trust you."

"Is my word good enough?"

"Damn you! You gave that to Lord Bokin," Tarn said, as fresh insults were thrown.

A thin smile crossed Grona's face. "Yes, I gave my word. My word that is part of the warrior code and my personal honour. One that I never, ever break. As so many are quick to condemn, let me remind them. I told Bokin that I would not allow the bad blood between us to interfere in this mission. Nothing more – nothing less."

Looking back, Tarn realised how carefully Grona had chosen his words.

"You are as clever as you are brave, but beware. You have seen my potency. Do not test my patience any more. You may continue as part of my company but I want your unequivocal word that you will follow my orders."

"Then I give you my word, but before you go I will answer your original question. Myracadonis had a symbol – the Horned Demon."

CHAPTER 6

AFTER A LONG discussion, Tarn and Prince Wren drew up their plans. Several riders had left to deliver the latest news to Lord Bokin, King Leofrick and Nasan. Tarn had requested more men be sent to him, as many as could be spared, to ensure that they could cover a wider area.

From the number of villages identified by Wren as already infected by the Horned Demon, Tarn believed that the 'plague' had spread farther than they could imagine. More mystery but less fact, he thought. Any shaman could be dangerous and all dealt in the black side of magic. As in any craft, some practised their art more proficiently than others. How good was this one, he mused?

Taking his time to explore all possibilities led Tarn to one inescapable conclusion.

He sent for his father.

"I need information and I need it quickly. You will take your chosen men and ride north to seek out any news of the shaman, for it is believed that there are Helg strongholds along that route. Observe and report back. Under no circumstances are you to engage with the Helgs. We need information, Grona, not dead soldiers. Do I make myself clear?"

"If you say so."

"I do, now have you eaten?"

"Not yet."

"Then feed well and fast. Take what provisions you need and leave as soon as you are ready. One more thing. I will lead the remaining troops north-east towards the Helg stronghold of Grimsand. You can find us there – or if we have moved on, I will leave the normal trail markers for you to follow. Do you have any questions?"

"Only one. Does it pain you when you lose control of your mind?"

"Only after, when I look into eyes of the dead, especially if they were kin."

Grona looked at his son, shook his head, gave a half-hearted salute and left.

Elsewhere, food disappeared into eager mouths, along with wine, ale or water.

Each man had his preference but all wanted a full belly.

The grass was poor, so the men fed their horses with oatmeal from their supplies and draughts of water from the brook. Being born in the saddle, the Temujin took over the duties effortlessly. Tarn knew better than to interfere. The horses would need at least two hours before they could be ridden, and the men of the plains would have the final say. Nevertheless he ate and drank rapidly. He had many duties to attend to, but before he could wish Grona and his chosen men well, they had ridden out of the camp.

With his father gone, a relaxed feeling overcame him and the rest of the company, for none felt the need to constantly look over their shoulders. Tarn knew how they felt as he spooned chewy meat into his mouth, relishing the taste. With his back to a broad tree he closed his eyes and thought about what lay ahead.

Wynne had also found a sheltered spot to eat his rations, seemingly oblivious to the noise around him. His mind wandered back to his beloved Gisella as he gently removed a small locket engraved with G & W from around his neck. Caressing the silver he wondered why the gods had taken her.

From his early years he had never said too much to the young girls. He could not understand them. But the boys he understood. Always a popular figure he would rough and tumble with all of them. After one lad fell from his back and broke his arm Wynne learnt to be careful, realising that with his size came responsibility. He thought more than he spoke, usually taking care in his actions.

A strange family lived in a *hole* not far from Lakeside, so the gossip said. Most folk avoided the place and the occupants, saying it was a pit of the devil. After years of wondering an intrigued Wynne finally decided to pay a visit, against all the warnings from his friends. A few weeks short of his seventeenth birthday, the rap on the door would change his life.

A girl with a wondrous smile greeted him. Dark brown hair tied with ribbons hung down to her waist covering a simple fabric smock. Although her face radiated warmth and mischief, he could not take his eyes from her cleavage. Her words would never be forgotten.

"Have you come to see me, or my teats?"

"I'm ... err ... visiting."

"I am called Gisella, and you?"

"Wynne."

"Then come inside, Wynne, before your eyes pop out and the devil devours you."

He had crossed the threshold and entered a home so packed with pictures, books and artefacts that items had to be moved before he could sit. The *hole* had been cleverly cut into a deep bank so that only two sides would be exposed to the elements. Logs burned within a huge stone fireplace sending warmth to the many inner chambers. Wynne noted the excellent craftsmanship of every door, chair and table. Gisella's father had made them all, but due to the local people calling them devil worshippers he had been forced to sell his wares in other villages and hamlets to the south. The innocent family had reluctantly accepted their fate and ignored those that snubbed them. Life remained peaceful but solitary.

It would be the first of many visits that Wynne would make. Her parents welcomed the giant with gentle hands into their home, and Gisella teased him out of his reticence. She felt safe in his company when she accompanied him into Lakeside for the first time. The initial personal taunts hurt, but thereafter the trips became less eventful. The family's redemption was complete on the day of the wedding.

Gisella took the lead in most matters, as Wynne seldom offered any resistance. He had never known such happiness – it made him determined to think more and argue less. The love of his life had known his every move and every thought, so squabbles died with a hug and kiss.

Although childless, they had been happy and then she died. A cut on her hip, infection and a fever.

He travelled as far as he could to seek healers, anyone with a gift. He had met a man known to have a hidden talent, but his power lay with the dark gods. Wynne refused to take the chance that Gisella might live in this world, but eventually die in permanent shadow. As much as he loved her, the fear of sending her into everlasting torment in the afterlife dissuaded him. Whatever his pain, he knew that Gisella would be at peace with her own gods. Yet after all this time he still questioned his decision, blaming himself for her demise.

Eventually the delirium took her. He felt useless as he watched her slowly and painfully pass away. He had sought comfort in the hills, away from his friends and her parents, trying to forget the pain. On his return he had thrown himself into any task that his lord required of him. Only Tarn really understood the medicine that he needed.

He closed his eyes and saw Gisella walking happy, untroubled, her hair blowing free like a cornfield. As a warm smile caressed her face she danced to the tune of freedom. A surge of everlasting love flowed through and over him.

With arms crossed over his jerkin, he felt at peace. Gisella was free.

Once the horses had recovered the company moved out, setting a steady pace. At first they all stayed cool as their journey took them through the edge of a forest. The scent of pine wafting all around lifted their spirits. Robins followed the band, seeking disturbed insects, and crows loudly announced their presence as the company passed.

All too soon they began to climb. The trail was littered with stones and several large boulders. Hot sun lathered the horses as they picked their way, and Tarn's men sweated. Jackets had been removed – some shirts also – yet all still struggled in the heat. Following the poor track impeded their progress. The constant bouncing of the horses caused bodies to ache. Apart from a few loud curses, not many of the company complained.

Tarn marvelled at the amount of snow on the majestic mountains as he rode along. The grey clouds, sitting high above with the gods, stirred his imagination in a way he could only remember from his childhood. White lines ran down the highest slopes as if the gods held the peaks in snowy fingers. The synergy between land and sky took his breath away and Tarn felt very small in such a huge world.

Not for the first time did he wonder if the gods favoured him and his family. With all of Tasmina's prayers, surely some would be answered, he thought.

Hour after endless hour they rode upwards.

After a full day's ride, with only two short stops, Grimsand emerged from the dust. It occupied a small ridge between two mountain streams and had a perfect view looking down the valley – a good defensive position.

Conversely the stronghold looked neither strong nor capable of holding back any reasonably sized invader. Wooden posts showed signs of rot, the gates also. None of the company believed that it could withstand any vigorous assault. Yet the masks of relaxation soon gave way to the steel of expectation.

Tarn immediately sent two groups of ten to ride out and approach from east and west. He would lead the main company up the long slope.

"Draw your swords men; bowmen to covering positions, watch the flanks." Only the noise of the horses' hooves could be heard as Tarn's weary company closed in.

No movement could be seen, no noise could be heard from inside. The fear of the unknown grew as they rode ever closer to Grimsand.

A soaring eagle startled the lead group as they rode the last hundred yards to the closed gates. On Tarn's command they spread out even further. The silence was more worrying than any challenge.

"Wren. Take some of your men to open the gate. Be quick about it as night will soon be upon us."

The Prince gave the orders, saluted Tarn, and rode forward, lethal blade in hand. He had been schooled in swordplay by a master and few men would last long in his dance of death. But the years of action had given Wren a wise head when he faced any danger. Tarn trusted his friend implicitly.

On approaching the wooden gate, it slowly opened, as welcoming as the jaws of a hungry lion. Wren trotted forward warily.

"It's an open invitation to a death party," Wynne said. "Let me go with Wren – you know he gets lost in a tavern?"

Tarn hesitated. He should lead, but Wynne had made a good point. Wren knew what to do, yet it could only help his cause if the big man stood alongside him. Besides, everything felt strange about this place. The silence. The lack of movement and now the wide open gates. This was abnormal. He had to be prepared for anything.

"Take six bowmen with you and take no chances … you big lump."

"Yes, my lord." Wynne mockingly bowed, grinned, and then rode forward.

From the banners waving on the hills to the east and west, Tarn knew that his outriders had taken up position. The full company had spread out in case of attack, so now it was up to Wren.

The wailing started as soon as they reached the gates. Wren could see men and women bowing their heads to the floor in supplication. Dressed in raggedy clothes, they cut a forlorn sight. Conversely groups of young men, dressed in leather tunics and brightly coloured leggings, stood around the edges, arms crossed, faces sneering. All had the curved scimitars that the Helgs favoured, whilst a couple held small axes.

The swords hung undisturbed in their scabbards but the axes nestled in tight hands. Wren cautiously moved forward giving orders to stay sharp and to cover any moves that the Helgs might make.

The town looked even more dilapidated on the inside. Rotting doors, badly repaired, swung on creaky hinges brown with rust. Cats and dogs fought over a pile of rubbish in one corner. A stink of decay hung in the air like a mist. Houses had been built with no semblance of order and all had been poorly maintained. Tied to a rail, several horses swung their tails back and forth trying to swish away annoying flies. Prominent ribs showed through taut skins.

The people kneeling looked similar to the horses as only the fighters could be regarded as being well-fed.

As Wren's troop looked around, a slow rumbling in the earth caused them to immediately cease all activity. A pulsating light appeared in the middle of the stockade, causing the townsfolk to move rapidly back from the heat. The light constantly changed colour until an outline formed. Bit by bit a demon emerged from the ground, edging upwards, alive with menace, the horns long and sharp. The rainbow colours held all spellbound, even those outside, as it rose higher into the air. Horses bucked in the air, throwing riders to the ground. Good men backed away as fear of the unknown assaulted them. Many looked upwards, clasping their hands together, imploring the gods to protect them. As the demon took shape the colours changed into reds and yellows, scarlet and ochre, as fire and ash spewed from its prodigious maw.

Now they had seen the Horned Demon.

"Stand firm." Those outside heard Wren yell.

As he watched the sorcery unfold, Tarn desperately tore his eyes away and looked at the forces under his command. His brain told him that, as Captain, he should stay outside the village. Conversely his heart urged him to move inside. Wren's abilities had been proven time and again, yet Tarn could not sit idly by. Something tugged at his inner-self. He summoned his thoughts. His heart won.

He ordered his first lieutenant Mellis, a trusty Bokin man, to take charge and to stay put, then trotted his horse forward into the dazzling light.

As he entered through the gates, coalescing white and orange flames rose from the ground in a dance of deadly beauty to lick at the Horned Demon. The soldiers looked at the spectacle unfolding before them, some unaware that a hidden shape grew deep within the inferno.

"You fools, how dare you pit your feeble strength against mine? You will all die."

The shaman had risen before them, clad in a long cloak of black and silver. Tall and arrogant, he held a short sword in his left hand and a book in his right. In the fading light, his whole body sparkled against the grey backdrop of the buildings. With a clash of thunder a bolt of lightning hit the tallest, starting a fire in the roof. Some of the townsfolk frantically stood up and ran for cover. Even the Helg warriors cowered under his gaze.

A hush descended as all eyes turned to stare.

Some soldiers quickly recovered their senses, saw the menace and ran forward to hack at the figure of evil. They died as wildfire spread from the shaman's hands. Wynne managed to drop his sword just in time as a blue flame ran up it, leaving the hilt and his hand smoking. Now fully roused, the rest shouted, cursing the shaman, eager for a fight. They moved closer.

Tarn had watched from the edge of his company, mesmerised like everyone else, but still with his eyes wide open. He had noticed complete inaction from the Helgs, both fighters and civilians alike.

"Stand fast men!"

"Now, back ten paces!"

"Flankers to the ready!"

The crisp commands triggered the soldiers' discipline.

Tarn stepped forward with a little more confidence. The Helg fighters, still standing around the periphery, would now be covered. The shaman would soon make the opening gambit in the game of war and Tarn guessed that he may be readying a surprise.

"What do you want, shaman?"

"Power, of course. Leaders lead and followers follow. I command the Helgs and they do my biding. What do you have?"

"The choice to decide our own fate. The choice of freedom."

"Ha! Ha! Ha! You puny people talk of freedom but what does it mean? No one is truly free, you pathetic fools. The beggar sits by the wayside as free as a bird but if he fails to eat he starves. So he steals to sate his hunger, is caught and sent to a dungeon. Is he free now? A husband beats his wife. She endures, for where would she go? Is she free? Your lord sits in a castle, collecting his taxes, so you all pay for his privileged position. Are you free? The lord has his power but mine is greater. You would do well not to overestimate your strength nor misjudge mine, most of which is hidden."

"You think this stinking hole is a good illustration of your power? I have seen less muck in a pigpen. Only those you have forced would ever follow you. Look around you shaman – all I see is sorrow and fear," Tarn said.

"I see obedience," Myracadonis said.

He sheathed his sword. Gazing in the air he opened the pages of the old and battered book. He held it open for those closest to see. The page looked brown and dry, crackling in the shaman's hands. In the centre a picture of the Horned Demon throbbed like a beating heart, growing and flowing upward from the page to merge with the lights above.

"The future," he said.

"Load of shit," Wynne retorted.

"We have met before, Tarn and Wynne of Lakeside. An attractive village … once … if I recall."

A snarling Tarn was never a pretty sight. Prince Wren moved to his side, a firm hand on his shoulder, whilst Wynne moved slightly ahead.

"Obviously you did not see me, being too carried away with your own self-importance. But who would have guessed that a simple village boy would rise to become a berserker? I made a mistake in underestimating you. It won't happen again." He rubbed his fingers over a small amulet on his left wrist. It blushed with yellow, causing the shaman to smile.

"Eventually your race will succumb, as the Helgs did. After you have declared your allegiance, I will sweep away the old order from the northern kingdoms and then conquer the south. All will follow Myracadonis, or die. There is nothing on this pathetic world that can prevent me from my destiny."

"By all the gods Tarn, this … Myracadonis is a lunatic," Wynne said as quietly as he could. Prince Wren nodded in agreement.

"I hear you children. If you play with adults, you must expect to be smacked and you are playing my game now. Only death awaits those that break the rules."

"Using magic to suppress a race is against the law of the gods," Wren said.

"Your gods live in the mountains, Prince Wren, whereas mine are constantly with me. Do you really think that I worry about your gods? I stand as tall as they do. Come visit me. I will offer you a warm welcome, no matter the time of year."

"Shaman, you are clearly mad. You are not a god nor will you ever be one. I will not bandy any more words with you for I see little sign of any real power," Tarn said.

"Pah! You know nothing. Why should I, Myracadonis, show my power against such a pitiful rabble?"

"Surrender and I guarantee you a fair hearing."

Mocking laughter filled the air. "Surrender? To you? Tarn … you must be the most stupid warrior that ever lived. You thought that you had beaten me all those years ago; you failed. And you cannot do it now. Prepare to die."

Myracadonis began to fade as the air thickened and a haze surrounded his robes.

"Come back and fight, you coward," Wynne shouted.

As soon as the shaman disappeared, the Helg fighters awoke, urged on by an endless chant from the invisible leader. They surged into action, leaping high in the air with a wax-like glaze over their eyes. More than thirty young men screamed like devils and launched themselves against the Stormborn and Bokin men. Several arrows struck the Helgs, yet still they fought, wildly slashing and cutting all in their path – including their own petrified townsfolk too slow to move aside.

Five of the company fell in the Helg onslaught before Wren and Tarn could stand before them. One diminutive but crazed Helg rushed towards Tarn, sword held high above his head. At the last second Tarn knelt on one knee, slashed his sword across the offered stomach and disembowelled the man ... yet even then he tried to rise. Milky eyes stared from the face of the Helg as Tarn cut the head from the body with one easy sweep. As more of the enemy advanced he thrust forward and his broadsword entered the chest of the first. A quick withdrawal, a parry and a slash and another Helg would never rise again. The remaining fighters stopped in front of him. Tarn slowly advanced as they waited. A cool rage grew hotter with every step that he took as the berserk warrior took control. Cut and thrust, the Helgs fell. Tarn's arm surged with power as he moved. Those that stood and fought died in a matter of seconds.

The voice of Myracadonis boomed around the enclosure. Only the Helg fighters understood the incantation as he sent new energy into their bodies.

Three crazed Helgs had simultaneously attacked Wren. His legendry swordsmanship had dispatched them but had failed to prevent several cuts and a deep gash to his arm. As more Helgs closed in, Stormborn bowmen rushed to his aid and sent arrow after arrow into the enemy. The chaotic scene echoed to the sound of steel and the cries of agony as, one by one, the young men of the aptly named Grimsand emptied their blood and guts on the battleground.

To Tarn's surprise, the last remaining Helgs turned their attention to the local populace. Bowmen loosed a few arrows but Tarn ordered them to cease, for the terrified people of Grimsand could receive a stray arrow by mistake.

The lunacy had to be stopped. Wynne stepped forward together with several doughty fighters of the Bokin Band. The eyes of their opponents, now bloodshot and as murky as a swamp, bore into them as they advanced.

Wynne yelled a battle cry and swung his huge broadsword; the Bokin warriors followed, slashing and cutting with deadly precision. Snarling faces screamed at the attackers as they swung their swords wildly into the melee. In less than a minute seven young Helgs would never see the sun again. All semblance of insanity had been replaced with the vacant eyes of the departed. Blood flowed freely, creating sticky puddles. Wynne and his fighters counted their cuts, glad to be alive but disgusted with the futile loss of so many young lives.

The monotonous chanting ceased. The remaining Helgs dropped their weapons, looking bewildered. Tarn's company held firm, seeking any sign of another attack. One by one, they pushed their swords back into scabbards. Sweaty hands wiped themselves dry on blood-stained trews, and arms wiped sweat from furrowed brows as the band cautiously relaxed.

"These are simply boys, Tarn. What manner of magic is this?" Sweat poured from Wynne's body, which shook with uncontrolled anger. Anger that grew tenfold as a member of the band turned over the body of a young Helg – a 'fighter' with a linen youth bracelet on his wrist.

"This boy is not yet old enough to wed. The bracelet proves he has not grown into manhood and now he never will."

Others examined the dead juveniles. Many wore a youth bracelet on a wrist but none looked more than eighteen or nineteen summers. The aftermath of any battle always created a wave of mixed emotions through the minds of the survivors. 'Dead men cannot harm you' had been the Maxilla and Stormborn saying for decades, and normally they felt little compassion for the dead, but killing young men and boys touched their hearts.

Tarn looked at the killing ground. He saw again his relentless slaughter of the Helg boys. Guilt washed through his body like a tidal wave. He vomited on the sand, sickened by his own actions that had cost the lives of so many youngsters. He looked to the sky for answers but the gods stayed silent. He walked away, holding his head in his hands.

Wynne strode forward and stood before all of the company. With his red face and huge body spotted with blood, he looked like a giant of olden days come back to haunt them.

"My brothers in arms, I swear on all the true gods that I will kill the shaman Myracadonis, and scatter his body and entrails to the four winds." He held his sword aloft, pointing to the heavens, the disappearing sun reflecting on the blade. "I am coming for you, shaman, no matter where you are."

CHAPTER 7

IN THE MORNING, the full details of the previous evening's battle unfolded. Blood stained the dirt, and the local villagers, almost all Helg-born, wept. The final count was forty-one dead and fifteen wounded, ten of whom had suffered serious injuries. Tarn's company had lost five good men, with another six unable to travel. The rest had cuts that would heal. Already the company doctor and his helpers had begun the work of burial, as well as sewing up the many cuts. Binding wounds with wild thyme honey gave the best for protection against loss of limb or even death. The men and women of Grimsand did nothing to interfere, preferring to remain in the background.

"By all the gods, stop that bloody wailing," a tired Wynne screamed. A sergeant was already moving, ready to offer assistance. I wish you luck, Wynne thought.

The clearing up continued. As slow as a donkey and as docile as a rabbit, was how one Stormborn trooper described Grimsand's population. They wandered, they stood and they stared with faces expressionless as a clean sheet. Every one of them had to be shown what to do and how to do it. To the soldiers they were training young children. But in a state of trance the unfocused eyes of the youngsters told the men all they needed to know.

The men searched Grimsand as thoroughly as they would look for a lost gold coin but they found no sign of Myracadonis, nor any of his belongings. He had vanished from the dirt and the grime, leaving his mindless followers behind.

The best structure was commandeered for the wounded. The doctor and his helpers worked hard to save lives. In the filthy conditions every table and medical implement had to be thoroughly washed. They drew pure water from the well and heated the metal tools in a fire.

The remaining locals looked on with disinterest before eventually gathering in a large hall. None of them complained and few even spoke.

The company men, afraid that the shaman might return, chose where to lay their belongings – some inside a building, others outside in the earth. As always, the Temujin stayed with the horses.

~~~

The nomadic Temujin loved their horses with a passion that their wives could only dream about. Wild stallions and mares roamed across their lands.

As and when needed, the wild horses would be roped and haltered in the great round-up. Each tribe would decide whether to use or sell individual animals. Once the traditional spit on two hands had taken place, all bartering ceased, the deal finished. Breaking a horse oath was punishable by removal of one hand, or rarely, the death of the oath breaker.

After all the formalities had been completed and the animals corralled in the correct pens the fun would commence. The leader would formerly announce the Gathering for an Equumess Festtumm. Folklore suggested that a wise man of another age had first used the name but, as few books from that era existed, no one really knew. Neither did they care too much as they loved the annual meet, and would throw themselves into a frenzy dancing to the beat of drums and small flutes. Very few outsiders knew of the Gathering, nor the location. Set on a plateau between two hilly ranges, Ylvester provided the perfect terrain. Steep hills covered in trees, tamarisk and spruce on the higher slopes, gave way to poplars, alders and a few elms in the more sheltered areas. The grass grew lush in summertime, the green mixing with an array of red poppy and thistle. And the huge cliffs at one end provided a cascade of constant water, screaming on its descent into a large lake. Ylvester – the wood land – welcomed them. Providing game for tens of thousands, feed for the animals and a constant supply of water for all, the Temujin cherished their vast oasis in a testing land. Apart from an emergency, no one dared to visit this holy place at any other time of the year. The sentence was death.

The merriment and drinking would last until dawn. And after a few hours sleep, they would rise, eat and prepare for the games.

The men would display astonishing acts of horsemanship as those watching shouted encouragement. Picking a spear from the ground at full gallop, then throwing it at a scarecrow target, defined the warriors – but sending an arrow into a moving target dragged by another rider would always be the ultimate test. Battle skills were hugely important when choosing leaders thus the young men of each tribe always did their upmost to impress.

Older men would place bets on the races as they drunk on grape spirit. Burning the mouth and harsh on the way down, Snakeblood left many a Temujin wondering what day it was.

Women dealt with the domestic duties. They drove the wagons and carts, covering long distances in their nomadic existence. Whilst all had horses, some families drove small herds of stringy cattle or even sheep. To keep out the cold the women would prepare wonderful stews using wild herbs of rosemary and thyme, amongst many others, to enhance the flavour. Their land was generally poor but good grasslands provided enough feed for the animals. Trading, especially with the Maxilla, ensured that none starved. Thin goats followed each family, the meat stringy but palatable, the milk refreshing. Occasionally beef or horse steak would be served. The calm faces of the women belied the fact that all could use a sharp blade if required. Hissing like cats, they frequently fought amongst each other when the clans met.

The plains leading to the harsh steppes had been their domain for centuries. Bitter winds could sweep across the bleak lands, yet in summer wild flowers burst into bloom everywhere. The Temujin nation loved the isolation and the beauty.

Wrapped in woollen shirts under leather jerkins and thick hairy leggings, they had learned to survive the unforgiving conditions. Long leather boots, made supple by their own urine, ensured comfortable feet. Surprisingly, men had chosen to shave their heads in some of the tribes, wearing sheepskin hats to keep them from cold. Sheep provided more than meat and warm skins for clothing or blankets, for the heat of their bodies warmed the Temujin in the winter.

The Temujin tribe had been small when a boy child had been born. They called him Nasan, the boy of life. Being unusually large in the womb, the birth proved difficult but the boy survived whilst the mother bled to death. It was one life for another.

From the infant's earliest weeks his father knew he had sired a special son. Nasan rode a horse six months before others of his age, and drew a bowstring completely back a few years later. The boy learnt fast – a sword, a knife – the skills to win and survive came easily to him. His father taught him how to detach himself from anger, to control his feelings and allow an opponent to display theirs first. Slowly Nasan absorbed the knowledge, changing him from a clever novice into a master craftsman.

He killed his first man at the age of fifteen. The Horsehairs, another tribe of the plains, wandered into their camp. They exchanged pleasantries, made a sacrifice to the gods, and a fine meal of goat meat and small vegetables appeared, filling the empty stomachs of both tribes. As his father would not return for two more days, Nasan, being the eldest son, took on the role of host. After the meal he offered all the men a cup of traditional Snakeblood, which instantly disappeared down thirsty throats. Some of Nasan's clan felt uneasy with their visitors and advised him to be cautious, as it was known that some would see an opportunity in the absence of a tribe leader. Nasan listened but ignored the idea of placation. Another word, carefully crafted into an insult, encouraged young Nasan to act. He boldly placed his sword and knife on a blanket and challenged Malasi, the leader of the Horsehairs, to a wrestling match. His opponent saw a youth as tall and as wide as himself but grinned wickedly at the pleasures that would await him after the contest.

They circled each other warily before the first strike. Nasan threw the chief in the air. He stepped back expecting the end of the contest but the man raced in again, yelling insults. A side step, a lift of a leg and Nasan's opponent fell once more into the dust. A long blade appeared in Malasi's hand, his eyes burning with intent. A shout and Nasan caught a knife thrown by one of his tribe. It was over in seconds. Malasi would never see another sunrise. An unanswered challenge and the Horsehairs became part of the Temujin tribe.

Nasan's father could not believe his luck when he returned. His tribe had almost doubled in size in less than a week.

As the years passed, so the Temujin tribe flourished. Nasan led in all but name, yet still deferring to his father. He had 'persuaded' others to join his tribe, awaiting the chance to implement his dream.

At the age of twenty-four he had dared to challenge and defeat the previous leader of all the tribes in a knife fight at the Gathering. The first to be badly cut would normally submit but, although bleeding profusely, his opponent refused to yield. A dagger in his belly soon changed his mind … permanently.

Nasan revelled in his victory and made plans for the future, for he had a vision. With all the tribes now flocking to the Temujin leader, the banner of the dark stallion would soon ride across all the plains.

The Helgs had often strayed to plunder the western tribes and the Nordmen from the Harsh Lands to the north would regularly try to steal horses.

Knowing that the southern lands had proved to be friendly in the distant past, he sent a delegation to King Leofrick and Lord Bokin. They reached an accord over trade. Food, materials, pots and pans, ale and weapons would be exchanged for the horses and ponies of the Temujin. Broken in, ready to ride, the horses proved invaluable to both the Stormborn and Maxilla alike. Only the feel of a saddle on their backs would initially cause them to rear up but, within a week, the horses would be ready. Some had even been bred with the faster horses of the southern lands. The result led to stronger, tireless mounts that could travel longer distances with a heavier load.

All sides honoured the agreements. Stormborn riders would not only send regular patrols along their border they shared with the Helgs, they also rode into Nasan's western lands – with his invitation. The incursions from Helg bandits had almost faded away.

But the bond with the Maxilla clan grew the strongest. Men of the Bokin Band became an accepted sight over the plains. It proved to be a double success for it not only provided a great training ground, but also strengthened ties. Nordmen attacks became less frequent as Maxilla and Temujin chased and harassed them back across the border. Rangers from the band covered hundreds of miles in pursuit of the enemy, with the various tribes providing appropriate information. Although the long rides would prove tiring, the men never wavered due to the welcome that they received. A change of horse was always available, along with a tasty meal. Only hot baths eluded them but dusty nostrils soon learnt to deal with the stench. A few of the band asked their lord to be permanently based in the lands of the Temujin, so much did they cherish the unyielding landscape. Bokin agreed; he held no desires to base any of his forces permanently in Temujin lands; but he guessed that the men were besotted with the wild young girls. No doubt they had married in secret having first proved themselves to the Temujin clans.

Not long after his accession as ruler of the tribes, the first real test of Nasan's stewardship reared up from the west. The Helgs invaded the lands of the Maxilla and surrounded Castle Bokin. Nasan sent more than a hundred of his bowmen to assist his new ally. Few returned but the bond between two nations intensified, strengthening his position with his own kin as well as with the Maxilla people.

Over the coming years, he convinced, bribed and used cold steel to force individual tribes to join together. The Plains had been the domain of so many individuals, but now they were the home of one nation. The Temujin ruled across a vast ocean of grass and sand.

Nasan ruled ably. His astute brain resided within a strong body, giving him an advantage over any potential usurper. Ruthless in his determination to succeed and wise in his decision-making, only a fool had dared to challenge him. That man died slowly.

The Temujin needed constant ruling with a mailed fist, as some warrior from a distant clan could issue a challenge at any time. Such a threat was unlikely, but Nasan dare not travel too far from home. His days of conquest had come to an end.

As the years passed, and the union of friendship grew, the time came once again for allies to assist one another. With the recent increase in the number of Helg raiders attacking his western tribes, news of a suspected attack against the Maxilla did not surprise Nasan. The

Temujin were not found wanting but with renewed pressure from the Nordmen, and fearing another challenge to his leadership, Nasan dare not send too many warriors south. Thus he urged Lord Bokin to maintain a detachment of rangers on his northern borders. Lord Bokin agreed on the understanding that Nasan would provide horses and as many bowmen as could be spared to face any new threat from the Helgs.

An agreement had been reached, although both prayed that the rumours would prove false. Neither wanted to see another Lakeside. The appalling loss of life and the devastation of that village could not be allowed to happen again.

~~~

The company gathered in small units as the last light diminished in the west. Fires had been lit and water boiled in pans as the aroma of hot food wafted around the yard. Men swallowed their food greedily, drank beer and water, and sharpened swords as they discussed the events of an unbelievable day. The stories always grew in the telling. Tarn and Prince Wren moved from group to group, answering questions and joking with their subordinates.

"Prince Wren ... is it true that once upon a time you made love to a buxom girl so ugly that she had to wear a sack over her head?" A Stormborn soldier shouted.

"No, Vernen, only a plain one with extremely large breasts the size of over-ripe melons. But she was still better looking than the last whore you bedded. What was the name of that skinny girl? Oh! Yes! Jenni for a penny. And you paid a full silver, or was it two?"

The soldier disappeared under a collection of items thrown at him, the laughter infectious.

"Get him an eyeglass." "Has it dropped off yet?" "Want a pretty goat for the night?" The insults flew faster than a kestrel.

"Poor ale, was it?" Tarn said.

"No," Wren replied, "poor eyesight."

The laughing continued, and they both chuckled. As they moved towards their headquarters, situated near the main gate, the forge looked as fragile as all the other buildings but at least it had a hole-free roof and fresh straw.

After a brief rest, Tarn stood at the slatted door to the forge. His eyes searched the heavens and the road to the open gate for signs of returning riders. Mellis had approached him a few hours before. He explained that standing outside the gate whilst a battle raged inside, did not sit well on restless Maxilla shoulders. The men were eager to prove their worth and he had asked Tarn for permission to send some of them on scouting duties, to seek any clues of recent horse movements in the vicinity. Tarn had agreed and now waited impatiently.

The rest of the company had been split. He ordered one group to guard the stronghold against outside attack, but the second had been called to assist, not only with guarding the local population, but also to help their injured brothers in arms. The remaining men would sleep and then replace their colleagues as ordered by their commanders.

As the dark of the night sky overcame any lingering brightness the wandering scouts reported back. Tracks from the rear of the village led up towards the mountains. Horses had travelled that way a few days ago, but no fresh marks could be seen. They had ridden all of the other trails for three or four miles with the same result.

Tarn thanked the lead scout Zavian for his report. He bid him take a small flagon of ale, bread and salted pork for each man and to ensure that the gate was securely closed before they ate their provisions. Zavian saluted and departed. Tarn pondered the news. Clearly Myracadonis did not travel on horseback, he thought as he walked back inside the forge.

He called a meeting with his trusted companions to discuss options. Wynne had agreed, then sat on the threshold, half in and half out, reluctant to decide where he wanted to be. Chewing on bacon rind, his mind wandered elsewhere. Mellis, Tarn's second in command, had joined Tarn and Wren inside. Wren's aide Althalos arrived a few minutes later.

They pulled together wooden benches, barrels, and a table, and rubbed the cobwebs and dust away before seating themselves.

"What a mess," Wren said to no one in particular.

"We know that the land is free from 'human' prying eyes, but what about the demon in the sky?" Wren asked, dipping his bread into meat fat.

"We have destroyed all the paintings of the Horned Demon, as well as several idols of the shaman. We have to hope that he cannot hear or see us. Personally I doubt that he can, for why else would he need to show himself for the … boys to attack us?" Tarn spoke slowly, as if thinking out loud.

"I agree with Tarn," Althalos said, clearing his nose from dust. Being the oldest man in the company his words carried extra weight. "I also heard tales of the shaman during the war, but refused to believe in his presence. This time I made it my place to know as much as I could, so I spoke to Grona before he left on his scouting duties. His only recollection was that the evil one's power appeared to fade with distance, hence seeing him from afar and living to tell the tale. Look what happened here; on his orders, the village boys acted insanely, yet once that incessant noise ceased, all the fire in their bellies disappeared. Was it a spell?"

Wren ran his fingers through his long hair as a constant stream of confusing thoughts rushed around his brain. "It certainly sounded hypnotic to me. Even now they are walking in a trance-like state. Let us assume that Tarn is correct. If we believe that he cannot see us, then we have an advantage, but what do we do next?"

Tarn walked around in a circle as he spoke. "We must discuss all possibilities. For instance, how do we cope with his magical powers?" Seeing only the shake of heads he continued. "There is something odd about this Myracadonis. He persuades others to do his bidding. Why? Can he not use his magic on us? He had every opportunity to do so. Did he not say 'prepare to die'? Yet here we stand after fighting and beating his young men. They died for him and he fled, leaving them to their fate."

"Our men are glad to be alive but there is little celebration in killing innocents," Wren said as he searched for his tankard of ale.

"Innocents with deadly swords," Althalos countered.

"Yet I pity the fallen all the same."

Tarn sat down. "I wonder if this shaman decided not to show us his strength?"

Althalos scratched his neck. "It may be a deliberate ploy but remember a good shaman needs magic but a poor shaman needs gullible men. I wonder which one threatens us."

"I have a theory," Tarn said. "I believe that this demon is more dangerous than Myracadonis. Destroy that and all his power will disappear."

"A plausible idea. Can you prove it?" said Wren.

"No ... so think about it. Other matters require our attention for now. What about our casualties? How many able men do we have?" Tarn asked, his voice husky. Wren passed the ale but Tarn declined, instead seeking a skin of water.

Mellis the career soldier stepped forward. From the age of fifteen he had served the Maxilla clan well. Once Tarn's superior officer, he now served him. The twenty-five year age difference was irrelevant. As he rose through the ranks he learned that sloppy decisions could lose battles. Tarn asked the right questions and made the right choices.

"We started with twenty-three of the Maxilla clan, and were joined by Prince Wren and fifty-five Stormborn. We are also blessed with twelve Temujin. Grona took four men to the north and we have lost five men with six badly wounded. That leaves a total of seventy-five, but that excludes those who must attend to our wounded as well as securing the village. Sir!"

"Mellis, what is the minimum number that we can leave in Grimsand?"

"Sir! Taking into account the walking wounded, I estimate twenty-five."

"That's not enough. We cannot fight these drugged-up lunatics, let alone Myracadonis, with so few," Althalos said.

"I need to ... what is it, Wren?"

Wren tried hard to wipe the smile from his face. "Alas my friend, my guilty secret is no more. When you requested more men from Lord Bokin, I knew that time would fly faster than they could travel. The message I sent to my father requested a full cavalry regiment be dispatched immediately. You know my father – always ready to oblige his favourite son. As their journey is much shorter from the west, then they should be with us later today."

A flush of anger flashed across Tarn's face as he heard the news, for the chain of command had been compromised. Looking at Wren's huge grin soon tempered his annoyance. A frown became a wide smile, which brought relief to a heavy heart.

Tarn offered his hand to Prince Wren. "Never let it be said that friends cannot keep secrets from each other. But next time perhaps you could release the news a little earlier."

"Timing is everything, my lord and friend. Have I not …"

The raised hand said it all but Wren ignored it.

"As you command Lord Tarn but before you speak further, you should know that the Stormborn regard you as a true lord, even if Lord Bokin fails to recognise the fact. But he will soon enough."

"Well done sir," Mellis said officiously.

"I think Prince Wren could be joking," Tarn said.

"Wait and see my friend, wait and see."

Tarn swotted a fly away. "Any more surprises, anyone? Good! So let us return to Althalos's comments. I believe that he could be right. Myracadonis has the power to hypnotise and control his people, but only those nearby. Over long distances that influence appears to diminish rapidly. But let us recall today's events. Myracadonis appeared, he spoke, and then his physical body vanished. The droning started immediately and the attack began. Clearly his presence was not needed for the Helgs to attack, but how close must he be? I have little knowledge of the magical arts but could he have left this place? The farther he flew the more his power waned … perhaps? How long did the battle last? No more than ten minutes, I suspect. Flying as fast as a bird would mean a short journey. A shaman's flight … who knows? But he cannot be too far away. Our dilemma – where will we find him?"

"Follow the Demon, perhaps," Wren said. "As we do not have a starting point then my suggestion sounds foolish. However we have not looked for one to guide us. Perhaps we should commence our search at the biggest town in the mountains."

"There are no towns, only villages or strongholds which are numerous," Mellis replied.

"We must start somewhere." Tarn could not prevent himself from raising his voice.

Wynne rose from his seat. Towering above them he pointed to the table, clearing it, before rearranging platters, tankards and anything else he could find to show a map.

"I have been thinking. Where would I live as a shaman amongst the Helgs? As we know there are no large towns or castles. Yes, there are many strongholds like this, for the people live far and wide … but no natural meeting place, except one."

Eyes dilated in anticipation.

"What, or rather where is this, Wynne?"

"Rope's End Rock. It meets all his requirements. Because of its position, hanging over the gorge, a small army could defend it." He pointed to his map; the waterfall, the deep valley and the landmass all made sense.

"How do you know of this place?" Wren asked.

"I listen. Two men visited the Castle Inn last year. They were joking about a strange place at the bottom of the mountains, a place where the people strung up prisoners on a hook high in the clouds. They called it Rope's End Rock."

"I have heard this name before, but have any of you?" Tarn scanned the faces. "So, Wynne, is this … 'map' … accurate?"

"Possibly, but I have another pointer, admittedly more tenuous. A friend of mine travelled there a couple of years after the war seeking trade. He found his way to the rock due to rumours of a growing population. The place surprised him for more people that he imagined lived in the caves. Some had fashioned crude wooden huts and cut holes deep into the bedrock to attach them securely, whilst others had cut into the rocks high above, enlarging caves and creating walkways. But the place reeked with the transparency of a flimsy curtain. He felt watched the whole time and departed as soon as he could. Over a good ale he told me the full story then drew a map of the rock and cave area. Being fascinated at the time, the name clearly stuck in my brain for it came back to me as you spoke."

"Good ale can do wonders for the imagination," Althalos said.

"And I have a long memory," Wynne retorted.

"Enough! It is indeed tenuous, Wynne, but can anyone suggest a better alternative?" Tarn looked at the shake of each head in turn. "So be it; we leave as soon as Prince Wren's cavalry arrive.

Mellis, take Althalos with you. Pick the men to stay and ensure that we have enough provisions for the trip. Strip the town if you have to. From here the ride should take us a day. One more thing … what is it, Wynne?"

"From your orders, Tarn, I assume that you know where Rope's End Rock is."

"Yea gods, I thought that you did."

"I do," a quiet voice said. One of the Stormborn guards walked tentatively towards them, cheeks red as a beacon.

"Speak up, man," Prince Wren ordered. Before the guard could commence,

Wynne thrust a pot into his shaking hands, urging him to drink. Wren's impatience bubbled over as the beer slowly disappeared down the man's throat. Throwing a glacial stare in Wynne's direction, he tried to control himself.

"Name!"

"Askoma, my Prince."

"Now, tell us what you know."

"Some years ago, three of us, all Stormborn, rode into the Helg lands for a bet. A long ride beckoned so we took provisions for more than a week. Some of the tracks are good, others not so, but we made it. All of us saw Rope's End Rock but one did not come back."

"Why not?" Wren asked in a more conciliatory manner.

"Becan disappeared. He simply disappeared. We tried to find him, Lord – we really did – but that place is evil. Our limbs turned leaden, our brains confused. The harder we searched the more our minds wandered as if someone was trying to corrupt, even destroy our souls. We had to leave, you have to believe me."

Tarn looked at this young soldier; he pitied him. He knew the Stormborn code. No one would ever leave a comrade unless absolutely necessary. "How old were you?"

"Fourteen, sir."

"I believe you. Can you take us to this place, so that we may … cleanse it?"

"Yes Lord. Am I to be charged afterwards?"

Wren interjected before Tarn could answer. "You have suffered enough; I can see it in your eyes. No lad, you will ride up front with Captain Tarn and your Prince. Show us the way and we will follow. Let us fight this menace together. Now find parchment and ink."

Clear details of the route quickly emerged as Askoma drew a detailed map. On finishing, he hastily withdrew. Wynne's map bore a passable resemblance to the one now before them. Althalos nodded an apology as a brief silence ensued.

"I trust in Wynne's and Askoma's memories," Tarn said, "and we will follow the trail to Rope's End Rock. I do not wish to be disappointed but I feel we are close to our goal now. By the grace of the gods, sharpen your sword, Wynne; you are likely to face your nemesis sooner that you thought."

"That's if Grona has not beaten me to it."

"What?" Tarn and Wren shouted together.

"When Grona left we travelled north. Rope's End Rock is now east of us. You sent him north-east. The route is difficult but if Askoma's map is true, Grona and his men would be travelling directly toward the rock. He could already be there."

"By all the gods, we must go to his aid," Tarn said. "We will travel fast and light, and as soon as possible. Mellis, you and Wynne organise the men. Tell them of our need for haste. We must leave at first light as I fear that I have sent five brave men to their deaths."

CHAPTER 8

THE MEN CHOSEN by Grona knew him well. They had fought with him, got drunk and whored with him. Lowis would argue with Grona, and anyone else around if he was in the mood. And, after a good session in a tavern, he could pick an argument with himself. His quick temper often stoked a fire into a raging blaze; his friends reluctant to join in and douse the flames.

Ammett said little, but had a way of speaking that calmed most folk, yet often ended up out of pocket when he was left to pay for the damages, caused by Lowis.

Grona ruled with an iron fist, but after so many years his men knew when to ignore … the stupid orders. It was rare for any of them to stray far from one another. And if they did it would always be for a warm bed and a hot woman. With so much practise, they developed a sixth sense about when to run from angry husbands or whorehouse ruffians.

Terryn would always be the first to offer a stream of sarcastic advice to his fellows caught with their pants down. Grona would simply shut his ears, threaten any interloper and continue with pleasuring the woman.

Whilst the others were enjoying night time escapades Eagle-Eye wandered, usually into a bed with two women. Being slimmer than his friends he told the women that he felt the cold more. Eagle-Eye was aptly named. When he sensed danger, he would rouse the others and plan a safe withdrawal.

Fighting or resting, Grona's men were as close as any band of men could be and as predictable as the rising sun.

All four of them rejoiced when they heard the news that Tarn had ordered Grona to ride out. Being out on their own with no outside interference suited them perfectly. Few secrets existed between long-standing comrades and with Grona in charge they knew the ropes. They collected their pay, took risks and fought to win, or die in the fight. And with Grona, they felt more comfortable than with any other commander. It meant a greater chance of survival.

The aged warrior had explained their mission and they had set out determined to show their worth, or at least find a good inn and a hot meal in trying. And if a whore or two came along, then so much the better.

Recent heavy rain had eroded the soil away and rutted the trail with stones.

Progress was too slow for Grona's liking, but even he had to listen to his horse.

Dark clouds had given way to sunshine before rain clouds appeared, a common occurrence in the higher hills. Rain would fall in torrents on an upslope, yet within a few miles on the descent, the land would be dry and dusty. Rain capes rapidly gave way to unbuttoned tunics. Unconcerned, Grona's men chatted away, enjoying the ride. They had visited several villages, all empty; the locals must have fled before they arrived. This raised even more questions in Grona's mind. How had they known?

They found abandoned food and ale, and although it was poor fare they ate and drank their fill. They destroyed any paintings of the Horned Demon or defaced them with horse dung. The monotony continued that day and the next with only the bickering breaking the silence.

As they rounded a curve in the trail on the morning of the third day, another mud heap of a village emerged through the dust. Crows noisily flew upwards, annoyed at being disturbed. A skinny dog gave out a long bark before disappearing behind a gap in an old lichen-covered wall. Grona and his men immediately searched for signs of human activity. As they began to dismount outside of a stone cottage, Terryn pointed. A man and a woman had run from the last house and across the dirt track, trying desperately to hide inside a hawthorn hedge. They trotted forward warily.

"Come out," Terryn shouted, his spear pointing towards them.

Lowis rode his horse to the other side of the hedge waving his broadsword.

As the ragged pair carefully emerged, blood dripped down their arms and faces, liquid gifts from the needles.

"Who are you?" Terryn demanded.

"Forgive us, lords. I am Korna, this is Fern. We are poor people, we have nothing."

The man wore a badly soiled leather tunic over tight leggings and a woollen undershirt. But his leather boots were long and bright.

Lowis pointed. "I bet a silver; he didn't buy those."

"Probably a thief then," Terryn said." And you know what happens to thieves."

With Eagle-Eye and Ammett on watch, the questions began.

Grona watched silently, happy to let his men have some fun after all the boredom. These two locals might even provide some useful information, he thought.

"Where did you get them?" Terryn said.

"I found them, Lord."

"Really! You think me stupid." A slim blade replaced the spear in Terryn's hand.

Drips ran down the man's face and mucus from his nose as he shook violently.

"It is true, Lord; my father found them a mile further along the track."

Sitting on the ground, with her head held low, the woman looked a forlorn sight. The thorns in the hedge had savaged her thin dress and shawl. Her hands struggled to keep them around her as she shook and shivered with fright. Dirty lines ran down her pallid face where tears had trickled. Rocking from side to side she would quickly dare to look in Terryn's direction, before returning to stare at the earth once more.

Lowis ignored her. He leapt to the ground and grabbed the end of one boot. "These are standard issue Bokin ranger boots. You bastard. What did you do to him?" A strong hand grabbed the man's throat, hauling him upright. He tried to reply, but choked; the girl intervened on her father's behalf.

"Please … he was dead when we found him. We gave him a proper burial." More tears ran freely. With pain and sorrow etched on her weary face, she could have seen twenty-five summers, but they guessed maybe sixteen was nearer the mark.

"Show me," Grona said.

She took them to the spot. A small mound of earth covered in rocks lay by the track on the outskirts of the village. Grona ordered the man to dig. The soil was hard, the grave shallow. The men tied cloths around their faces as the body appeared, decomposing but still in one piece. The girl wept. The stench assaulted their nostrils. The ranger had not been in the ground for very long, and had been buried with his clothes intact – but with no papers, identification was impossible. Unsurprisingly none of his weapons could be found, although the arrowhead lodged in his chest confirmed the cause of his demise.

Grona wondered whether either of them had been involved in the killing. But he also wondered why a murderer would carefully bury the body and then place a small posy of wild flowers on the grave. Had she told the truth? Ordering Korna to rebury the corpse, he pondered. He needed more answers. When her father had finished the gruesome task, the girl replaced the flowers.

The men of Grona's band recited a short prayer before standing tall to salute their fallen comrade.

"What happened?"

Korna still rubbed his bruised throat yet looked him straight in the eyes. A good sign, Grona thought.

"Our village once thrived. We sold the best honey in the hills, the abundant wild herbs giving it a special flavour. But the number of bees in our once thriving hives began to fall. Hard times from the past had emerged once more. One morning a man of magic appeared offering food, shelter and silver, enticing most of my neighbours away."

"And why not you?" Terryn demanded.

"Many were hungry. We were not, but his words did not ring true." He paused. "Amazingly, after a full year of the seasons the number of bees increased."

His daughter shook in disgust. "I hated him. Those evil lustful eyes followed me everywhere."

"How long ago did he leave?" Grona said.

"Nearly two years. We have been pestered by his followers ever since. Lord … that is why we hid from you. The others will not return until you leave."

"What others?" Terryn asked.

"How many and where are they?" Lowis demanded.

"We are few. Our hidey-holes are unknown to each other."

"You will … "

Grona cut in. "Forget it, Lowis – that's an order. What about the ranger you buried?"

"Our hives are mainly on the southern slopes. By the time we moved to the north and found his body, some days had passed since he had died."

"Where was his horse? Did you hear anything, perhaps war cries or the sound of swords clashing?"

"The horse tracks were several days old. The man lay adjacent to the track, the body cold and decaying. We buried him, prayed to the gods and returned to our labours. We could do no more."

Grona rubbed his hands together, letting his mind mull over the options. He believed part of the story. A horse could carry a dead man for miles before stopping, and the lack of papers could be down to the ranger's leather sack being lost, but the absence of the horse and weapons troubled him. Rangers rode strong steeds, well trained and valuable, and weapons could be sold easily in any market place. Grona believed that these two knew more, but any girl that placed flowers on a stranger's grave had a good heart. He could persuade father and daughter but his real interest lay elsewhere. Time had moved on and he needed to move with it.

"This magic man, did he have a name?" Grona asked.

"Myracadonis," the girl spat.

"And where would I find him?"

Korna spoke. "You should head to Harlan. They will know the way."

"And the boots?" Terryn demanded.

"Forget it," Grona said. "They are too small for any of us anyway." Terryn raised his head, grinding his teeth as hard as he could. Grona ignored him.

After a meal of roasted goat with herbs, Grona prepared to leave. He exchanged a packet of salt and some dried beef for five jars of honey. Korna led the way out of the village, pointing to the correct track.

"Whatever you think, Lord, the boots were a gift from a dead man. We do not steal."

A long ride awaited them as they followed Korna's route. It looked old and unused. Long grass covered hidden rocks and stones, keeping the men constantly alert. The horses plodded on regardless. The winding track steepened within a few miles, making their rate of progress slow even further. Doggedly they pushed on and upwards, their bodies already aching. The hours passed slowly.

Clop! Shit! Clop! Clop! Shit! The horses stumbled, the riders swore. Afternoon changed to evening as the sun began to fall over the distant mountains.

After a further hour of tedious plodding, Grona decided to call a halt for the day. They set up camp in a small hollow by a fast-flowing stream as the sun's rays finally edged over the snow-tipped peaks. They drew lots for the first watch before bedding down for the night.

Grona dreamt of a large house built on the banks of a rapid stream. A lovely woman smiled as he laid four fresh salmon alongside his fishing gear. A glass of Maxilla red appeared alongside him as he sat in a chair, stretching out his legs. The scent of fresh jasmine wafted around him whilst he disappeared into a world of harmony.

Eagle-Eye twitched constantly, whilst Ammett lay as still as a corpse.

Terryn looked at the four snoring bodies, wishing that he too could dream as they did. But when Lowis screamed out in his sleep, he thought better of it. He would awaken Lowis first.

Apart from a large owl hooting loudly in the trees above them, all five warriors eventually slept, some better than others.

Whilst eating their breakfast Grona unfolded his map, showing the men the route. Their current track was not marked but Korna had told him that it would save a day's ride. He had readily responded to questions about Harlan – Hard Land in the old tongue – providing as much detail as he could remember from his last visit. Grona had a sixth sense about anyone lying and in this case he believed him, for Korna simply wanted his band to leave as speedily as they could.

The small but important village of Harlan lay some five miles ahead. Korna had said that it was situated on a crossroad of two tracks and that travellers would frequent its infamous tavern and stock up on supplies. Other races, as well as Helgs, lived there. News, good or bad, should be readily available.

The news of a tavern brought a raucous cheer from his men. Ammett the Quiet as he was sometimes known loved his ale more than food.

He suggested a long session of drink and food to ease the soreness from their arses. On hearing that Grona would personally cut the liver out of any of them found drunk, his yells of approval disappeared in an instance.

Five silent Bokin warriors pointed their horses along the track for the short ride ahead.

As they rode in, the numerous groups of armed Helgs gave them cause to keep their swords at the ready. Harlan appeared to be a place where men wishing to survive took extra care. They had seen this scene many times before, yet still a degree of anxiety remained. But they had laughed when Grona ordered them to act naturally as travellers seeking to replenish their provisions. They split up. Grona told them to keep their eyes and ears open and re-join each other in the Heartland tavern within the hour.

Harlan proved to be a disappointment and a surprise for Grona. The tavern served weak beer, but the travellers were all eager to talk. Grona invited them to join his small table and paid for the ale. Loosened tongues wagged away and he listened, taking a few gulps along the way.

It soon became clear that the number of travellers had been dwindling for many months - fear had driven them away.

"I always feel relaxed after an ale or two my friends, but something is nagging me." The travellers looked at each other. "You see, I may have some business with the leader of this pig-sty, but who is he?"

A thin faced man braved Grona's glare.

Evil Never Dies

"Be careful of the boys, they run the place but he ... is never far away."

"You have aroused my curiosity friend, who is he?"

"Shoosh! He is called the shaman but his real name is Myracadonis. And now I must leave, I have said too much."

Grona grabbed his arm. "And where do I find this shaman?"

"Go to the granite rock ... and he will find you."

Scurrying away he tripped over a chair leg. His fellow travellers rushed to pick him up. Grona frowned as the door closed behind them.

Grona could read the signs, he knew that Myracadonis held this village in his sway. He could see that the local business folk, Helg and incomers alike, pragmatists all, hated the militia and the shaman. They were bad for business.

Grona's brain whirled. The village held an important secret, he was sure of it. What had he missed? The more he thought, the more it eluded him.

On stretching his legs he looked out of the tavern through a faded glass window. He grimaced at the reflection of his weather-beaten face. What happened to the years, old man? Then he smiled. Where were the older men? He had not seen any male between the ages of twenty to sixty. The missing piece of the puzzle was staring back at him.

He stepped outside and took a short walk to stretch heavy legs. The dowdy surroundings, the dust and the grime, reminded him of Townend, another village on the edge of the mountains but far away in the land of the Seafarers. The same worn out look, but they knew how to enjoy themselves and the good times had been many. Compared to that southern town this place couldn't organise a smile, let alone a party.

A few structures were built of stone but most were of timber. The scent of pine followed him as he walked through the village. The ring of metal struck by a hammer caused him to ponder why there were so few horses. A squealing pig ran out of a side alley, chased by a small man holding a stick; the former easily outran the latter. Years of neglect and indifference hung in the air like a fog. Grona watched the locals carefully. Walking along with heads bowed they ignored all contact with anyone else. The reek of stale sweat on their bodies, leather trews, and jerkins stained with dirt, made him blow his nose and spit as he passed. Only the watching militia stood tall. In their groups of threes and fours they waited and watched. His battle-hardened eyes missed nothing, Grona had seen enough. He retraced his steps. One by one, his men joined him in a quiet corner of the Heartland Tavern.

"You first, Lowis."

"Little business. Low stocks. Discontent. Fear everywhere. The boys hold the power in the village. All fear the shaman."

Lowis certainly knew how to summarise in a few words, Grona thought. Pity it changed when he'd had a flagon or two.

"What about you, Terryn?"

"I agree, aged one, yet there is more to this place. I felt a presence watching me and my skin still prickles to think about it. Evil lives here, you can be sure of it. But I'll tell you something I saw no true warriors. Most of these boys don't know how to wipe their arses, let alone wield a sword."

As the laughter died Ammett and Eagle-Eye made their reports. The conclusion was obvious. Grona made his decision.

"Time to earn your pay, boys. Follow me."

Terryn looked to the heavens. "Here we go again. Why do I follow this old bastard?" he said quietly.

"At least my hearing is still intact," Grona retorted.

He led them to the granite rock, pulled down his trousers and pissed on the image of the Horned Demon. Laughter resonated around the rock as his men duplicated the act.

"Myracadonis," he shouted. "Come show yourself."

Some of the young men ambled towards them, uncertain of what to do.

"Are you afraid of five old men, shaman?" Grona roared as loudly as he could.

The Horned Demon began to pulsate as dazzling white light flowed freely from the mouth.

Terryn took a warriors stance. "To the right, old man. The babies are looking for a fight."

"By all the gods, I only age him by two years," Grona said to himself as he strode to the front, his faithful companions spreading out to stand either side of him.

Nine young men charged like maniacs, swords held high above their heads.

The first fell instantly to Grona's swinging blow, his head landing next to his body. Terryn's axe clove through the torso of the second. A sword pierced the lung of the third but still the young Helgs rushed forward. In minutes all nine lay dead at the feet of Grona and his men. They stood firm, blood dripping from their weapons. Lowis wiped the blade on his trews and said a quick prayer, readying himself.

"Bloody amateurs," Terryn said.

"Agreed," Ammett said.

"Myracadonis, you send boys to do a man's work. Face me, you coward," Grona shouted.

Lowis pointed. "More are coming."

They braced themselves, eager to do battle, confident in their abilities.

The earth shook, throwing everyone off their feet. Flashing lights continued to cascade from the Horned Demon as the shaman stood before them.

"So 'Father' Grona, you come to my lands, desecrate my idol of the Horned Demon and insult me. Now you issue a challenge. You are truly pathetic."

Grona picked himself up and met the shaman's gaze. He thrust his broadsword into the ground, crossed his arms and spat on the floor.

"Are you a mirage? Or are you real? And don't call me father."

Myracadonis briefly hesitated. "Stupidity must run in the family. How your race can believe in besting me is beyond arrogance. Your son has already pitted his strength against mine. I doubt that you can succeed where he failed but it matters little, for you will die one way or another."

Grona's thoughts turned to Tarn, yet not believing a word from the mouth of Myracadonis. "It matters to me you whoreson. Stand before me like a man, not by magic."

The image faded into a riot of colour. A flash of light and a 'solid 'Myracadonis stood before him.

"Now we fight, man to man, winner takes all. Sword, knives or bare hands, whatever you wish you piece of shit."

Grona thought he saw fear in the shaman's eyes, the fear of a dead man. That was all he needed to rush forward and grab him by the throat, his huge hands pressing into the slender neck. As the gurgling started his hands encompassed empty air and he knew that Myracadonis had tricked him.

"Ha! Ha! With your brawn against my magic, there can only be one winner. The noose is tightening around your slender necks, not mine, but now is not the time of your demise. You have dared to challenge me openly and thus I dare to respond. If you have the guts, 'Father' Grona, follow me."

An eerie cry rang out. "See you at Rope's ... End ... Rock."

"Shit!" Grona said.

"Where did he go?" Terryn yelled.

The ever-watchful Eagle-Eye shouted a warning. "More boys are approaching, maybe twenty to thirty."

Once again the five stood together as the young men ambled towards them. The scared youngsters looked from one to another. One brave soul ran forward, waving a large sword that he could barely hold. Using little effort, Lowis disarmed the boy before a backhand across the face left him whimpering in the dirt. Another ran towards Grona. A strong punch in the mouth sent him sprawling. Leaving the boy to count his teeth, Grona stood before the others.

"Enough! You cannot beat us. If you continue to fight we will kill you all. This is your last chance. Who leads here?"

A tall slender lad, holding two daggers, stepped forward. Terryn removed them before he could cut himself.

"We are not strong enough to kill you now, but the shaman will return and our strength will grow."

The aged warriors looked on with disinterest.

"I am Grona. Now, what is your name?"

"They call me Jemson, leader to you."

"I admire your arrogance, but a leader of what?"

"We will be strong and … right the wrongs that you and your … kind … have done."

All five warriors exchanged looks.

"You think that you can beat us, farm boy?"

"One day we will."

As usual, Grona did the opposite of what his men expected.

"Fighting always makes me thirsty. Terryn, remove all their weapons. It is time to talk over a tankard of ale."

"You are not going to kill us," a small lad said.

"No. This is your lucky day. We only kill children on Tuesdays." Grona placed his hands on the boy's shoulders. "Listen to me, all of you. Myracadonis has filled your heads with lies. It is time for you to know the truth, to listen and to make a choice. It is time for all of you to grow up."

By the time they reached the Heartland tavern, more than forty youths were in tow. Crowding them all inside proved difficult. The old warrior organised mugs of ale for all of them, no matter their age. Standing or sitting all drank and relaxed.

"Drink up, lads, it'll put hair on your chests," he chortled.

Over the next hour he told them the full story. The invasion of their kin-folk into Maxilla lands, the dreadful battle for Lakeside where over five hundred people on both sides perished and the final battle two miles from Castle Bokin. Interruptions gradually ebbed away as eyes widened in shock. Grona left nothing out, including the gory details of how so many women and children were murdered. Several lads had to rush out. The smell of vomit drifting through the door of the inn did nothing to calm queasy stomachs.

"Any questions?"

Too shocked to answer, most of the youths lowered their heads, whilst the braver souls glared malevolently.

Jemson stood up. "I … am not good with words. We have no teachers, our fathers left before we could learn. Is this a … story-dream of that day? Did our fathers kill so many or do you lie?"

"I do not lie," Grona thundered, crossing the fingers on his right hand. Well, not often, he thought. "This is no dream, boy. It happened as I said."

"You speak big words but cannot prove them."

"I told you, I do not lie."

Several boys spoke. The ale had loosened tongues. "How do we know?"

With his hand immediately covering the hilt of his sword and eyes afire, the nearest boys backed away from Grona.

"I should cut … but maybe that's for another day." He fought to regain control over his raging fury. Slowly it began to dissipate but the questioning eyes still burned into him.

Grona moved to face Jemson eyeball to eyeball. "Now what did that whoreson promise you?"

"The liquid would make us strong. The Horned Demon would protect us but it only worked if he was close by."

"Go on," Grona urged.

"He said we would be invin … never lose. All would be able to kill many men."

"And what had we done to deserve this … punishment?"

"You had stolen our lands. The good lands to the south."

"And your men and your mothers, what did they say?"

"Only the very old men still live here. We learnt to ignore them. The women were said to be evil. The young ones should only be used for pleasure, the rest avoided."

"Where did your fathers go?"

"None of us knows. He … told us they were doing his work elsewhere. The women say they are dead, they remember them once a year, but they are wrong. You are wrong. Our fathers will return one day."

Grona had heard enough. "All of you go home. Speak to the old men. Ask questions. Listen to your mothers and you will learn. One more thing. You have no teachers, no fathers, because they will never return. Go! Now!"

Groans issued from open lips, unbelieving stares from wide eyes. Grona knew that brainwashing could not be cured over one beer, yet the insolence and concealed fury still took him a little by surprise. Must be blaming me for the deaths of their fathers, he thought.

"One moment, children. Clearly you are not as clever as I thought, so I will repeat myself one last time. You have a simple choice to make. Carry on believing and acting the way that you are and you will be dead within a few weeks. Armed warriors will arrive and they will show you no mercy. The alternative is as I said. Listen and learn or die young. Now go home."

"I wish to learn … the truth, but not here," Jemson said as the last of his friends left the Heartland tavern. Grona looked at the slim frame, the face without stubble and the trembling hands. Yet there was something more to the youth. He sensed that behind the eyes a different Jemson lingered.

"It is good to learn. I am a man of many seasons, yet still learning; but what makes you think that the truth can be found away from Harlan?"

"I don't know, but there is nothing for me here."

Grona closed his eyes. The beginnings of an affinity with this lad reared its head inside him. He admired his arrogance, his leadership and lack of fear. The way he had openly challenged them showed potential. Jemson would perhaps make a good leader, if he lived that long. Thoughts of Tarn ran through his mind like a fresh breeze. If only, he wondered.

"Bollocks to that," he shouted. His men looked up. "Nothing," he said.

"How far can Myracadonis control you or others?"

"Not far. He has to face you in his own body, otherwise any control … goes … fades with distance and time. The nearer his … source, the more powerful he is." Jemson stood tall in front of Grona. "We are weak. You are strong. I want answers. Take me with you."

Lowis and Terryn looked on in surprise. The lines on Grona's old face deepened as a deep frown crossed his forehead.

"The shaman mentioned Rope's End Rock. Is that his stronghold?"

"Yes. The right track will save you ten miles and I can show you the way."

"You are needed here. Tell me where it is and you can start bridging the chasm between young and old and men and women."

"I know something else, something important. Let me go with you or … "

The old warrior weighed up the options. He needed to push on as quickly as possible and local knowledge could save precious time.

"You win. Give me the details and, if they please me, you have my word on the bargain." With right hand extended, Grona shook the hand of a young man quickly growing into a semblance of manhood.

"Myrac … him … he told us of an evil Lord. Name of Bokin. He said that he would lur … lure him and his men to Rope's End Rock. Here they would meet their gods. Then all their lands would be ours."

"Time to pray, Jemson. Prepare yourself – we leave in one hour."

A brief silence ensued as Jemson walked away. Then all the warriors spoke at once.

"Why take the boy? He's a liability. We can find this rock on our own, old man," Lowis said.

"I don't trust him either, Lowis, and if needs be I will cut his throat in an instant. However, we do not have enough time to wander aimlessly."

"Pah! It's a clear trap, Grona. What if Tarn's men are heading that way? We have to warn them," Eagle-Eye said.

Terryn countered. "It's an ambush alright but we don't know where they went. One of us should ride west to find them."

"And weaken our numbers in the bargain?" Lowis said.

The last man took his time as Grona patiently awaited his views.

"All roads for a warrior lead to Hell for none of us live forever, yet I would like to choose the place of my demise. To split up would be a waste of good companionship. We should ride together with this … boy, fight and die if need be, but the rule of this shaman must end. I am ready."

Grona burst out laughing, followed by the other three. "That is the longest speech that I have heard you make in thirty years, Ammett. By all the gods it was worth waiting for. How can I not agree with you? However, I believe that the invitation from Myracadonis has probably been given to my son as well. From the very beginning, we have been played like a fish on an extending line. The hearsay, the information that Prince Wren supplied, the almost *staged* fight here, the challenge to meet at Rope's End Rock, it all makes no sense but perfect sense. But there is one other piece of the puzzle that we have missed from the very beginning. How did Folmar Metton manage to escape from the clutches of this lunatic? You saw the state of his body and his mind; he didn't have enough energy to piss in the wind. No, the shaman let him leave to deliver a message. We are being enticed to his gathering in the hills and you know how much we all love parties."

"Any comments?" Grona said as he saw the frowns.

"Only one," Terryn said. "It's another first, old man – you used the word *son*."

Did I now? I must be losing my mind, Grona thought.

"Get ready to ride, you cowsons."

CHAPTER 9

IN THE LATE afternoon sun, Prince Wren's cavalry regiment of two hundred and fifty heavily armed men arrived. Hearts soared as they rode in and loud cheers erupted as three score Temujin bowmen, together with a number of spare horses, arrived some fifteen minutes later. Tarn immediately briefed them, and urged them to be ready for a departure in one hour. The men complained – not for themselves but for their horses. Advice from the Temujin had been reasonably positive, so Tarn stood firm. Tired horses would be exchanged for fresher mounts they had brought with them and Tarn was thus prepared to take the risk. He had agreed with Wren that Myracadonis would not expect them to ride at night. Luckily a new moon would show its blue face and light up the track that led to the rock, but nevertheless it would still be a long night.

In the fading light they set out.

The ride of the three races had begun.

Following the stars and guided by Askoma, with Wynne assisting, the company made slow but sure progress. They were allowed one brief stop to check on their horses and stretch tired legs but apart from that the company rode on. Tarn called a halt a few hours before dawn, for the men needed rest even though Rope's End Rock could only be a few miles away. He immediately ordered all to sleep, apart from the sentries. The company must have been weary to the bone, for the men gratefully sank into their blankets and pulled them over their heads to keep out the cold. Within minutes loud snores could be heard all over the encampment – enough to wake the dead, Tarn thought.

Tarn called a meeting of his senior soldiers and outlined his plans for the morning.

"Myracadonis must know where we are. Either he attacks now or he doesn't. The men are eager but need rest. More importantly, without fresh horses we cannot go on. But with refreshed mounts tomorrow will be different. I will ride in with half the mounted men. Scouts to both flanks with half the bowmen. The other half, together with the mounted Temujin bowmen, are with Wren. It will be up to you to decide if and when to attack."

"I have a better suggestion," Wren said. "Let me be the bait for Myracadonis. You can gauge the next move from his response. The speed of our horses can take us from any danger and, besides, you ride a horse like a drunk. You'd probably fall off if you galloped."

Tarn did not wish to relinquish responsibility but, although risky, Wren's idea made sense. The Stormborn spent their lives in the saddle.

"So be it. In the morning take fifty riders and draw him out if you can. If not, then ride like the devil. Now we have other things to discuss. Wren saw no warriors in the Helg villagers – likewise in Grimsand – there were only boys playing at soldiers, old folk and women. Could it be that all the warriors are hidden away at Rope's End Rock, or … "

"You mean, they all died in the war," Althalos finished for him.

"Not all, but it's a possibility that many perished as we chased them all the way back to the mountains. You may recall the bloodlust of our men." Tarn looked northwards, seeking answers to impossible questions.

The big man followed his gaze. The splendour of the jagged peaks tore at Wynne's heart but the clean air washed his soul. If only time could stand still for a while, or be reversed, all would be different, he thought. We could all be as pure as a newborn babe. A sharp intake of breath brought him back to the present, his brain functioning, but not yet in warrior mode.

"Tarn, I will follow you tomorrow, but I fear that this shaman may stand before the very gates of Hell." He walked slowly away, seeking solace in his blankets under the tall pine trees.

"I know how you feel, my friend," Tarn said sadly. But Wynne had already disappeared from sight.

Prince Wren and Althalos left to seek whatever sleep they could.

Mellis remained, seeing the sadness in his Captain's eyes. "He has a troubled soul. There is nothing you or anyone else can do, sir."

"Gisella?"

"I believe so. I have often noticed Wynne staring at the locket as if in a trance. He sits alone deep in her world wishing that he could join her yet not having the courage to do so."

"I had not noticed. How quickly we change in times of war. My brother is troubled and I ... I am too busy to help. What type of man ... have I become, Mellis?" Tarn bowed his head, holding it in both hands, his eyes closed.

"Captain ... Tarn, listen to me. I have known many men who have served Lord Bokin over the years. Most have been under my command; a select few, my superiors. You are the only man that has achieved both. Do you think that happens by chance? You are an uncomplicated man, easy to read and a joy to follow. All know that you would rather be at home with your family – we all would – yet you readily protect your clan without any complaint. You wish to protect all of us, even that miserable bastard that, alas, is your father."

"Yet in times of war I have this hidden talent, my curse."

"A berserk warrior yes you are, but accursed no. How you manage to separate the emotions of extreme love and extreme violence is beyond my understanding. Nevertheless, men will follow you to those gates of Hell if necessary for many have seen you fight. The berserker inside is mostly held in check. Rarely do you plumb the depths of evil and allow this to erupt. No lad, you are not afflicted, merely too gifted and too caring about those you lead. In this case Wynne's deep sadness affects you deeply yet there is nothing that you can do."

"But when my mind leads me down that foul path, I forget everything. I make no conscious decisions; my sword, my hand, arm and body are one. I try to remember but at the same time, wish to forget. Unforgiving faces interrupt my sleep every night. In my dreams, thousands scream at me, demanding vengeance. Wives bleed for their men folk, children wail with hungry bellies. As pain sears through my head, a bright light slowly grows in the deep black. I can only stretch my arm. The rest of my body refuses to move. Longer and longer my limb extends like a trail of wispy smoke and I am almost able to touch my salvation. At the last I hear a women's voice, as soft as doeskin and as gentle as a meadow breeze, and the words are forever the same."

"You will be tested, be patient, and be ready Tarn."

Mellis raised his eyes to the heavens. "You are truly blessed by the gods. Do you understand the meaning of her words?"

"I wish that I did. When Tasmina came into my life I began to pray to Jade, for who else brought us so close together? Maybe she has a plan for me? Or perhaps it is simply an endless nightmare?"

"The gods work in ways that we do not understand, even though we sometimes think that we do. Tarn, on the day of reckoning you will be judged fairly. Have you ever invaded another land, led a rebellion or killed an innocent mother or babe? Of course not! All men are flawed; it is in our nature. If we were perfect then we would be gods riding across the sky. You have killed where necessary yet saved the lives of so many. Mourn the dead, even the evil ones, but don't let it eat you away, lad."

Mellis moved towards Tarn and put a leathery hand on his shoulder. "Be assured, Wynne will not take his own life for he believes in the gods. He knows that he will never find peace if he commits such an act. Remember also that he has made a vow to kill this shaman and, given the chance, you know that he will succeed. You only have one life lad, live it. You're a long time dead."

Thoughts of dying without seeing Tasmina and Lori again tore through his head. Their happy voices reminded him of a life free of violence. Was his talent a gift from the gods, to protect those he loved? Did Jade, the goddess of love and harmony, listen to Tasmina's hopes and his own plea for peace?

"I will think on what you have said. Thank you, my friend."

As the blankets covered his body, Tarn closed his weary eyes. Fear and rage, self-hatred and loathing, love and understanding, even panic – the emotions flooded his weary mind. He tossed and turned like a ship in a storm before his body eventually yielded to slumber.

Darkness surrounded him as he found himself standing motionless in a cavern dripping with water. Rivulets had formed, sending the muddy liquid into unseen crevices. Plip! Plop! Plip! Plop! The noise reverberated off bleak stone to disappear down a threatening tunnel. Then the nausea started. Pain grew inside his head, clawing with passion at his brain. Covering his ears and shutting his eyes achieved nothing.

As some feeling returned to his sluggish limbs, Tarn shivered, his breath misty in the air. He walked further into the tunnel and his eyes grew accustomed to the dim light. The wail of a banshee pained his ears, threatening to deafen him. A wall materialised behind, forcing him forward into another, slightly brighter cave. Bats dropped from the roof to fly around his head, chattering in anger. His boots crunched on the mass of their dried droppings. The wail diminished as soft voices moaned in the distance drifting slowly towards him on a current of air.

"Murderer!"

"Killer!"

Images of his battles at Lakeland appeared, and Tarn fell to the floor. Limbs flew into the air as his blade cut and smote those that dared to face him. Heads lay severed on the ground, their eyes open, accusing. Dead bodies lay in piles all around him and fresh blood sprayed into his face, sticky and coagulating. The screams of the dying tore into him. He buried his face in his hands as the faces of his enemies screamed vengeance.

"What do you want from me?"

"Revenge!" The voices trailed away, leaving a silent cavern behind.

"By all the gods, please … leave me alone," Tarn cried.

A tiny golden orb appeared above his head. As it enlarged a dazzling light sent beams into the cavern and the darkness into oblivion.

Tasmina sat on the end of their bed, hands clasped in prayer, head bowed. Tears flowed from bloodshot eyes, leaving stains on her cheeks. She stood and walked around the room, making small adjustments to the furniture. The pillows on the bed needed fluffing but one needed something more. She pulled it close to her face and deeply inhaled, the silent sigh noticeable.

She left the room and moved to the main door. Lori played with another child in the small garden. She waved, and then continued with her game, her face aglow with the gift of innocence. Tasmina returned inside to sit in the larger chair. Caressing the wood and the covering, she ran slender fingers through her dark hair as she closed her eyes.

Tarn watched spellbound. All attempts to reach out, to speak, had failed. He watched and waited as helpless as a newborn lamb.

A shape emerged in one corner of the hearth, slowly solidifying into a naked human form. Long amber hair covered a slender back. As the naked woman turned, violet eyes glowing with intent looked straight through Tarn. His body trembled with apprehension and pleasure at such a pure form of womanhood. He could not turn his eyes away and, as if reading his mind, the face continued to look in his direction.

The woman moved towards his wife, running her hands through the same hair, carefully pushing the strands back from Tasmina's eyes. She kissed her forehead, smiled, looked once more at Tarn and vanished.

Immediately a dark cloud fell over his eyes as the tears fell once more.

A man of fire stood before him holding a huge sword in his left hand. In his right he held a skull full of maggots and beetles. The skull grew flesh as eyes of black filled the empty sockets and long wispy hair grew on the bony head and face.

The image changed. A boy sat outside a stone cottage, playing pick-up sticks with another. Behind them vegetables grew in a neat garden. Sitting on a wall, a man and a woman chatted, taking bites of red apples in between silent words as they did so. A large dog ran towards them, its long floppy ears flapping from side to side.

"Choose!"

A scream, a pull on his back and light gave way to darkness. Tarn awoke with Mellis standing over him.

"By god, sir, I thought you dead."

Tarn felt as if his bones had turned to jelly and his brains to mush. Soaked in perspiration, he smelt like an old boot covered in mould.

"I'm still alive, Mellis. Why did you wake me?"

"You ask why? You were screaming your head off, crying, not even breathing." The words tumbled out.

"A bad dream, nothing more. I will sleep now."

"If you say so sir," Mellis said doubtfully.

Tarn lay back on his hard bed and tried to make sense of the nightmare. He felt like a man caught between good and evil. But was he not a man who had committed both sinful and noble acts? Was this a test? Was it a reminder that all acts incur consequences? Who was the man with the skull? And the images of his family? His head began to pound with the endless possibilities.

As his tired eyes closed once more he remembered the words of Mellis.

"You only have one life."

But was now the time to change anything?

CHAPTER 10

As WHITE AND grey cumulus drifted above, Myracadonis wondered whether the gods looked up or down on the clouds. He allowed a thin smile to spread into a grin as he considered his past. Under the tutelage of Titian and his friends he had proved to be an adept and quick learner. Whatever task had been set, he had passed … eventually, even though the lesser deities placed many obstacles in his way. From the beginning he had expected to be praised for his efforts but it soon became apparent that any approval would be minimal. With a life of constant pain he had easily endured the punishments meted out for his regular failures. Yet, as his brain opened up to the teachings and constantly expanded with fresh knowledge, he found that his mistakes and the subsequent torments from his tutors ebbed away like an unwanted tide. His first attempt to conquer a land had proven futile. He had felt mentally ill-equipped to complete the task Titian had set, but his arrogance had overridden his feelings. As he remembered his failure any vestige of a smile vanished. Titian's punishment had been severe. His life had been forfeit yet somehow he had survived. Myracadonis knew that he had been lucky but even after all this time the memory made him angry.

He dragged himself back to the present and once more his face showed a trace of a pleasurable emotion, albeit a sneer, as he thought of his recent campaign. All was going to plan and he would achieve the tasks set by Titian. He would not fail this time. Myracadonis had already made plans for the future and any new powers offered by a grateful god would prove useful. Feeling satisfied, he looked upwards, eyes burning like the sun. He spread his arms, embracing the gods far above, sending them a message of his obedience.

He had sent out many patrols into the northern lands of the Stormborn and Maxilla. His orders had been explicit: kill any that crossed their way and destroy all buildings and animals. Use salt to render the fields useless and rape the women in front of the children as they would be more malleable thereafter. And always burn and burn again, for smoke would climb high in the sky. Many would guess the reason and the terror would spread.

He stroked his face with a dry hand as he turned his attention to the soldier in front of him. With the dust covering his tunic and trews, the man swayed gently from side to side, his mind wandering and his voice shaky. Even the blood, still dripping from a freshly opened cut on his right arm, did not change the attitude of the shaman.

"The reports are good. Your rewards await you in your hovel. There are two; choose which woman you require then send the other to your subordinate."

As the soldier departed on unsteady feet, Myracadonis's face shone with the delight of a man in ecstasy.

He felt exceptionally pleased with the latest information. Stormborn and Maxilla had been drawn to battle, but they had spent more time looking after the refugees than actually chasing his fighters. Many of his men had perished but the shaman cared little for numbers. There were plenty more disciples ready to take the place of the fallen. They just didn't know it yet. But when he took full control of these lands they would eagerly bow to their new master, all begging and all eager to please.

Only the troops sent into the lands of the Temujin had caused disappointment as virtually all had failed to return. The few that had, spoke of Helg warriors being staked into the earth over anthills, then left to die in the heat of the sun. He grinned, vowing to remember that torture for future use. Nevertheless, the panic had started and many tribes had moved away from their western borders. More Temujin warriors patrolled that area than before, but with the vastness of the lands, Myracadonis knew that he could send additional roving bands at any time. Let them tremble and let them wonder where I will strike next, he thought.

The seeds of fear and discontent had been truly sown.

And in the future he had other ways to spread terror. The recent memory of a daughter being urged to cut off her parents' arms and legs one by one, due to their failure to worship him, filled his heart with glee. Such was her gentle nature that the rest of the village believed her actions to be the will of the gods, and thus converted immediately to his cause. Little did they know that she acted under a spell from the book supplied by Titian. Afterwards she remembered nothing, apart from the later agony as he took her virginity away, raping her over and over again.

He rubbed his hands together and a glow flushed his face scarlet. Yes, he thought, and if all else fails I can bring down the wrath of the Horned Demon. Now that would make me happy, but I doubt that my enemies would enjoy the consequences. The thoughts bounced around his mind as his smile widened once more.

"The power is mine," he yelled into the sky.

As he held his head up high he decided that his future looked as bright as the noonday sun. The cunning plans that he had laid were drawing the fools ever closer. His enemies had received snippets of information, all hard earned, and all designed to carefully lead them to their inevitable fate.

His stomach churned with anticipation as he considered the arrival of Tarn and his company. Let them come tomorrow, he thought. I will be waiting, along with quite a few of my most fervent followers and I am sure that we can offer a surprise or two. After all I have planned this day for such a long time and it is only fair that they join in. He shuddered with the expectation of success.

Shaking with pleasure he raised his arms once more into the air, his body leisurely turning around in a full circle. He dabbed his moist eyes on the sleeve of his gown before bowing to the far away gods. Dark words issued from his mouth as he uttered a vile incantation.

At last, satisfied with his work, Myracadonis turned his attention to other matters. A young girl dressed in a tiny tunic appeared by his side. He immediately laid her on a slab of rock and cut the flimsy fabric from her body. Little bumps covered her arms and legs as the breeze gathered pace, yet she neither moved nor spoke. As the shaman's hands caressed her slim form, his voice began to rise in pitch, uttering strange words. The girl began to answer in the same tongue causing the shaman to move faster around the stone. Louder and louder they spoke and faster and faster Myracadonis moved, his robes flowing in his wake.

As one, they stopped, and the shaman looked down on his victim. He took a dagger from the slab and drew the blade along his forearm before offering the blood to the lips of the girl. He repeated the process but this time it was her blood that ran freely for him to suck. He sliced open her other arm, drinking her life force needing it more than she did. A froth of red covered his lips and face as his hands squeezed more from her arms. At last he stood above her, his face alive, his body sated with her salty blood.

He kissed her lightly on the lips and held her hand as she rose unsteadily on thin legs. Her hands softly rubbed the numerous scars on both arms as she wobbled her way back to the cave.

Sitting on the stone he felt weary beyond belief, yet satisfied with his efforts. Even Titian would be pleased with his success so far. Fresh virgin blood was now flowing through his veins, joining with his own, sending new energy into his body. And in the morning when the two had fully merged his energy would drive him forward to success and his ultimate ambition of becoming a demi-god.

CHAPTER 11

TARN ROUSED HIS men a full hour after dawn. Tired warriors fought poorly on tired horses so Tarn had ordered a late departure. He knew that an extra hour or two would be beneficial for his company but even so he worried about Grona and his men. If they had arrived before them, it could be too late anyway. Sacrificing his weary men was not an option so he ensured that they would be fully refreshed before their day of reckoning. Warriors fight better on a full stomach, he had been taught, so the cooks ensured a hearty meal for all the company. Jokingly, some of the men called it death by poisoning but warm fat over one fool's head soon stopped the jests.

A draught of water or a strong tisane and the outcome became inevitable. A steady stream of men entered the forest area designated a toilet. Bowels and bladders emptied whilst some stomachs forcibly ejected their contents. The growing stench did little to assist later arrivals.

As men prepared for battle, impatience grew and tempers flared and even little things preyed on frayed nerves. A perceived slight, an accidental bump of bodies, even a look could provoke a verbal, sometimes physical attack. Fear manifested itself in different ways. The men hated waiting; all were anxious to get on with the job.

Tarn called the company together.

"Stormborn, Temujin and Maxilla, we are united in this fight against evil and I am proud to stand with you. This evil that many of you have faced before. Only a fool would be unafraid of what lies ahead and none of you are fools. A long way from home we may be, but this growing disease will soon spread unless we cut out the heart. And that's ... enough rubbish for one day."

The men stayed quiet, wondering what was coming next.

"My friends, I promise you the party to end all parties once this is over. There will be enough food and drink to make you sick for a week and our fine leaders will pay for your pleasure."

Men jumped in the air whilst others banged swords on shields. Yells of hope and expectation carried on the wind as those farthest away joined in.

"And if you need a good whore, well I won't be the one telling your wives," Tarn shouted over the din.

The noisy mob shouted for all their worth.

"I go to kill this shaman, this Myracadonis. Who is with me?"

On a roar of agreement the whole company surged forward as one, their petty squabbles and moans forgotten. He had them now.

Tarn needed every man so there would be no rear-guard to look after the spare horses and kit as the company finally set out. Rope's End Rock would soon show its evil face and the men were itching for a fight.

Tarn led the way with the company following close behind. The shouts of approval slowly receded as minds turned to the possibility of death. Only the horses' hooves could be heard as they neared their goal. The shaman would know of their coming, yet as deep thoughts occupied their minds, tongues stayed quiet. Many said a prayer to the gods and all hoped to survive the battle.

After half an hour the sides of the valley began to close in. Steep slopes, covered in fir trees and sparse vegetation, loomed on either side. Carried down by the winter storms, many stones and other debris covered the trail. They slowed to pick their way round a fallen tree. Birds flew from the trees as they passed and giant eagles soared high under a light blue canopy, their all-seeing eyes seeking prey. Some of the slow-moving riders felt like rabbits. Perceived threats from all sides grew in their minds. Grey-black stone exuded menace and the company saw threats behind every tree and every rock. Tarn felt no need to give orders for bowmen had already notched arrows and swordsmen held their small leather shields at the ready. The gorge beckoned around another bend so none relaxed.

A spur of rock, lower than the others on the right-hand side, protruded from the cliff. As they approached, the trail bent to the left and a clear view of Rope's End Rock emerged. A figure swung from a rusty iron hook way above them.

Tarn knew the brown clothing as he had worn a scout's jerkin on many an occasion. The initial silence soon evaporated into anger as men swore, yelled and shouted at the disgusting cadaver swinging in the wind. Discipline quickly returned as a few harsh words kept the men in order.

"Time to see if you can ride as well as you boast, my friend," Tarn said. He shook Wren's hand and looked deep into his clear eyes. He saw no fear, only eagerness. "Good luck! Go!"

"And to you, my brother," Wren said.

As he trotted his horse towards the mouth of the gorge, Wren's company followed. Tarn feared an ambush so ordered bowmen and flanking troops to dismount and spread out along the lower slopes with the riders trailing behind. Moving forwards took longer than expected, as the ground dipped and rose in disorder with rain-washed gullies everywhere. Others followed, holding the horses' reins of those on foot. Tarn's dilemma grew and he urged haste as the main body followed Prince Wren far too slowly for his liking.

CHAPTER 12

A DRIZZLE FELL as the horses stumbled down the scree, hooves fighting for any grip that they could find. Fearing a fall, Grona and his men held the reins as tightly as they dared. Jemson had initially led them over firm tracks that meandered upwards. Then he led the way along a narrow ridge with a sheer drop on both sides, before the ride descended into a mass of broken stone and gravel.

"Shit! Shit! Shit!" Lowis said.

For the countless time, Grona shouted at Jemson. "Are you sure this is the way?"

"It is the way."

"It had better be, boy, or I'll have your guts for a necklace."

"God, my arse is sore," Terryn moaned. "Whoa, boy," he yelled as his stallion almost threw him.

As each horse picked its own path the stress on them increased in tandem with the riders. Sweat poured off the men and lather gathered around the necks of the horses. Staying in the saddle was all that mattered but more than once a rider lost his balance. Luckily, neither man nor beast suffered serious injuries, but the bruises would grow blue and ugly in the coming days.

"How much further boy?"

"Close now. Time to be quiet," Jemson said.

The land flattened. Jemson waved his hand, indicating a halt under a small wood of fir and scrub. "No talking," he whispered. He led the way along a stony path and through some thick bushes, then paused, pointing.

Grona and his men lay on the ground, looking directly towards Rope's End Rock and the previously hidden waterfall. A clear picture of the battlefield lay before them. They took in the lifeless body of a ranger swinging in the wind but they also saw the troops below. The Helgs had massed a small army at the northern end of the gorge, where a wide flat area stood. They could not be seen until any attackers had navigated the sharp turn at the southern end. As the trail narrowed at that point, mounted warriors would be forced to slow, compacting together. Once around the bend, it would take time for them to revert to their fighting wedge. The Helgs had chosen the ground well.

Jemson had pointed out the trail that entered from the south and now directed their attention towards the concealed pathways, one at either end of the gorge. Grona paid careful attention to the northern path.

"Where is that bastard of a shaman?" Grona said.

Eagle-Eye looked to the west. "I see something moving." The others followed his gaze but saw little. "There. Along the valley. It must be Tarn and his company. They have some way to go to the turn in the trail and the junction with the southern path. If we ride now we may be able to warn them."

"I see them, Eagle-Eye," Grona said.

All eyes focused on his hard face and his deep frown. The old warrior searched deep inside himself, hesitating, but not for long.

"Ammett, you will ride down. Ensure that they understand what awaits them."

Without any comment Ammett ran back the way they had come.

As he departed Terryn spoke. "And what do we do … aged one?"

"Well, my lucky lads, we are going to be heroes."

A small damp stain soiled Jemson's breeches. One eye developed a tic and his hands began to shake.

Grona took a bottle of yellow liquid from his pack, took a quick swig, then passed it around. Each man grimaced as it hit the back of his throat. After Jemson had vomited, Grona explained exactly what he had in mind.

CHAPTER 13

S‍UNSHINE STREAMED INTO the edge of the gorge, highlighting the swinging man. Wren ordered his men to approach in triple file, the maximum for the width of the track. "Keep the space," he ordered.

Another bend lay before them and Wren sensed that his destiny awaited him around the corner. He prayed that the bowmen would arrive on his flanks, even though he knew it to be a futile thought for Tarn needed them to protect the main company. All seemed quiet except for the snorting and clinking of the horses.

A faint thundering noise assailed their senses. The men pushed conical helms ever tighter onto damp heads, the nose guards rubbing on skin and gristle. They gripped their reins tighter as free hands withdrew sharpened swords from scabbards. Salt ran freely into peering eyes. Another few paces and Wren's company rounded the corner.

"My god," Wren said.

Armed horsemen galloped towards them. He took in the ranks of the Helgs beyond the riders and the wide space before him, realising that it was a perfect killing ground. But the Helgs had missed a trick, for in their impatience they had charged too soon.

"Stand fast, front ranks spread out. Althalos, do not come forward – stay with the other ranks at the narrow pass. Send word to Tarn immediately."

"But my Prince …"

"Do as I say. You have to hold the men together until Tarn arrives."

With that, Prince Wren rode slightly ahead of the Stormborn warriors, flying the royal standard of King Leofrick. His battle cry echoed in the canyon.

"Stormborn never die! Stormborn never die!"

His riders took up the chant.

With the gap only wide enough for six or seven horses, Wren felt that if he could hold the oncoming horsemen for ten minutes, then he had a chance – especially as the trail narrowed behind him. He saw his father again, standing in the great hall of Castle Stoke to give his blessing as he left. After all these years King Leofrick had finally forgiven him for his disobedience. "I will make you proud," Wren said to himself.

His cavalry sabre slid smoothly from its scabbard and he lifted it high above his head. The polished blade gleamed in the sun.

"Stormborn never die!"

CHAPTER 14

AMMETT RODE AT breakneck speed down the dry slope. His horse slid, nearly throwing him off on several occasions yet still he held on. Not only eager to deliver his message, he wanted to ride back and re-join his comrades in arms. It was safer that way.

At last the track flattened; he screamed at his horse and to the gods, cursing everyone and everything. As he forced his horse to gallop even faster, his legs and arms moved in different directions making him look like a raggedy scarecrow in a storm. Dust swirled in the air. A coughing fit took him; a deep hole shook horse and rider, yet still he remained in the saddle.

"Come on girl," he yelled.

A slight rise, a dip and he saw the main trail ahead of him. Alas, from the cloud of dust, he could see that Tarn's company had already passed.

"Arseholes. You're too bloody quick," he shouted as he yanked at the reins, urging his tired mount on. A madness possessed him but anger and fear drove Ammett on. After only half a mile the rear of the company came into view. He whipped his fading horse savagely across the back, urging every ounce from the mare. He screamed obscenities, pushing and shoving his way to the front.

"Tarn … Captain, it's a trap."

On delivering his report, he dismounted and patted the neck of his exhausted horse. Ammett watched the beast's head slowly fall, never to rise again. Tears fell from his worn-out face as he sat with his head in his hands. Horse and man had been friends for a long time. His task finished, it was a time to remember, for he had nothing else to give.

Tarn took instant action. "Crowlin, five men are to stay here with you as rear-guard. Look after the spare horses and provisions. Bowmen to the front now, swordsmen behind, everyone to ride. Follow me."

A frustrated Crowlin chose the men and deployed them immediately. As the main company rode like a windstorm, the rear-guard covered their faces from the huge dust cloud and cursed loudly. None of Crowlin's men appreciated the task when all their comrades would be fighting for their lives less than a mile away.

Tarn feared they would be too late as he charged recklessly forward. Even the sight of one of Wren's men riding towards him failed to slow him down, because he knew what terrible message he carried. The company galloping behind him found it difficult to keep up.

CHAPTER 15

PRINCE WREN HAD been slowly pushed back as one after another of his kin fell, cut down by the endless number of attackers. No Helg boys this time, he thought, as he parried another thrust with an aching arm. As fast as he dispatched one, another one or even two popped up. Memories of previous battles with more accomplished Helg swordsmen came to mind. Many of these Helgs swung wildly, untrained in swordplay. Untutored yes, but he knew that any blade could kill even in the most inexperienced of hands, and in this confined space, the smallest slip would mean certain death.

More than half his men had perished. Of those still fighting, all had sustained injuries, including the Prince. Although covered in blood from head to toe, and with numerous dents in helms and shields, the Stormborn continued to fight. Their tremendous courage knew no bounds as they stood like granite against the mass of bodies all eager to cut them down. Wren felt extreme pride in swinging his sword alongside them, yet he knew the signs. They could not last much longer. They had retreated to the narrowest point, but unless Tarn arrived very soon, they would be overcome. Even with Althalos's men filling the gaps from behind annihilation loomed.

Another parry, a flick and a jugular spurted red mist. A young Helg tried to unseat him from behind but as rear hooves lashed out the boy fell with a smashed skull. Space opened in front of him so he rode his horse into the gap, urging his dwindling band to follow. He had to give Tarn more time.

A huge ape-like Helg ran towards him, swinging a club like a small oak. All had fallen to his incredible power. He swung once more and it bounced off Wren's shield, denting the metal and breaking his left arm in the process. The Prince watched helplessly as the shield slipped from his grasp.

"You bastard," Wren said as he ran him through. The Helg fell under Wren's horse but another took his place. A lunge, a swift riposte and another opponent met his god, crushed under the weight of men and hooves of the horses. Agony screamed through Wren's body as his useless arm desperately held on to the reins. He continued to swing his sword, then steadied himself as a lull in the fighting appeared. A wry smile lit up his face because no archers had ridden forward. It soon disappeared as he counted only fifteen Stormborn still able to fight; the rest lay trampled in the scarlet dirt. Heroes all, Wren thought. I salute you.

"Here we stand, men. No retreat. I am proud to be with you. May the gods be kind."

The mass of bodies in such a confined space had to be removed before the Helgs could launch another attack. This had given both sides time to regroup, to pray and ready themselves. With so many Helgs pressing in, Wren sensed that it would be his last battle.

The men of the mountain advanced, yelling for death.

"Stormborn never die!" Bloody swords beat on battered shields.

"Helg! Helg! Helg!"

"Stormborn to me."

Swords clashed together, steel on steel ringing in the air. Triangular metal shields embellished with the Black Hawk received blow after blow as they bore the full force of the attacks. Grunting, groaning men struggled to stay alive as the screams of the wounded echoed around the gorge. Men tried to push back entrails into their stomachs. Arms left bodies as swords cut through flesh and bone. Some screamed for their loved ones, the dying cried out everywhere but the dead heard nothing as the butchery continued.

"One last hold, Stormborn. Stand firm. Watch that axe. Fight me you bastards, fight me." Prince Wren's speed defied belief. His sword hand flickered like a serpent's tongue. Each time it moved, a body fell to the ground. The ballet of death had arrived at Rope's End Rock but even his incredible speed could not prevent additional cuts from appearing all over his body. Fresh blood ran freely down his chest and dripped onto his stained breeches.

The Helgs saw the signs and struck with renewed vigour.

"See! He weakens! Forward!" they yelled.

Another blow to his helm, and without warning an assailant yanked the reins of Prince Wren's horse from his useless hand. His arm screamed in agony and his head throbbed with pain. He perceived small fairies darting around his body, leaving a trail of sparkling dust in their wake. He lifted his sword feebly in the air and tried to swat away the fairies attacking his horse. Shaking his head cleared some of the multicoloured specks from his eyes, but the images blurred into each other as he blinked rapidly. Surrounded by ghostly warriors, he thought of his wife and children whilst awaiting the inevitable.

Time slowed. A vision of a slashing double blade held in the hand of a warrior with ice-blue eyes flooded his mind as the battle axe stuck home.

CHAPTER 16

ON ROUNDING THE bend Tarn could see the mighty fight that had taken place. Bodies lay everywhere, most of them Helgs. Flies already buzzed, descending onto the corpses already being looted by the ghouls. He had seen the axe cleave into his friend's torso as if in slow motion. His cries had died to a whisper as eyes misted over. The fearless killer had arrived – too late to save a friend, but in time to exact terrible retribution.

The first wave of Stormborn cavalry engaged the mounted Helgs and pushed them back, creating space for those behind to fill. Maxilla men, led by Mellis, followed closely behind widening the fighting area. Temujin bowmen impatiently waited their turn before dismounting in front of Tarn. Draw and loose, the deadly shafts flew, creating a buzz in the air. Draw and loose again – a second wave rose before the first had found their soft targets. At a range of sixty paces, the Temujin arrows could not fail to punch deep into flesh, even with the lesser power of their hunting bows.

The Helgs were a mixed bag. Some held poorly made wooden shields, centred with an iron boss and with an edge of metal to protect from splits, whilst holding short stabbing swords in their other hand. Others held leather shields backed with wood, axes, and wore greaves but no other protection, whilst some wore rusty helms and held spears. The older and more experienced fighters carried the scimitar and displayed quality shields of wood. Those apart, all of the weaponry looked old and uncared for. None displayed any coat of arms and inexplicably no decoration or image of the Horned Demon. The few Stormborn had fought a battle against a far superior number of men and nearly prevailed. Alas, a rag-tag army with inferior weapons and armour had overpowered a disciplined force with sheer weight of numbers.

Tarn relied on strength and power. He saw the enemy as a deadly malignancy that had to be eradicated. Archers stepped aside as the berserk warrior urged his horse forward. Marvelling at his unique abilities did not prevent them from keeping well away from a man possessed. Helg after Helg fell to his deadly blade. Arms, legs and heads lay severed as he relentlessly rode forward. Those that frantically tried to move away from his reach speedily met their maker as Stormborn cavalry, led by Althalos, cut and thrust in unison to his left. On his right, Wynn surged ahead of Mellis to lead the Maxilla men, sweeping his mighty broadsword like a scythe. More arrows flew overhead as the Temujin watched for Helgs breaking from the melee.

Tarn's seasoned warriors, armed with sharp swords and protected by quality shields, cut deep swathes into the Helg ranks. The wounded begged for mercy but none was given.

The Helgs began to fall back, slowly then more speedily. Tarn's warriors screamed obscenities as they moved after them. Disciplined troops marched together in strong formation, stepping over swords, knives and other items thrown away in panic. Deadly faces and hard eyes picked out individual targets. Bowmen sent another volley into the retreating men. Revenge for the loss of their Prince and Stormborn riders burned deeply into their hearts which made them even more determined to win.

The retreating army suddenly stopped to gather together in the middle of the plateau. Loud cracks, like the sound of whips, could be heard as a poor defence line grew. Tarn and company hardly paused for breath as they advanced.

On Tarn's command every bowmen stepped forward. He ordered them to draw and loose and at such close range every arrow found a target. Leather shields could not stop them whilst men with wooden shields fared better. Man after man fell, screaming for their mothers. Another volley, more slaughter and Tarn ordered his bowmen to stand down. Both he and his swordsmen were itching to fight. A few Helg arrows flew towards his company, but Tarn's men held their shields high so even fewer embedded themselves into soft skin. The attacking swordsmen barely hesitated as they continued to advance, stepping over the fallen without a second look. Nothing could stop the march of death and the Helgs knew it.

The berserk warrior, sticky scarlet and gore dripping from his jerkin, motioned to his men to spread out. Once the encirclement of the enemy had been completed, the carnage and total annihilation of the enemy would commence. A spear landed in the ground before Tarn's feet. He dropped his polished shield to pick it up. Advancing on the group of soldiers, with his sword in one hand and his spear in the other, he clove through the front ranks as if cutting reeds in the lake. Only the bravest dare look him in the eyes, let alone fight. Althalos began to outflank the Helgs on the left, whilst Wynne's men destroyed those closest to Tarn.

A man swung an axe and missed. Wynne stepped neatly aside and almost cut his body in two. Another Helg ran forward hesitantly, stumbling in his fear. A Maxilla sergeant thrust his sword through a gaping mouth. Wynne covered the man as he pulled his sword free.

Tarn thrust and parried like lightning, oblivious to those around him. Friend and foe alike tried to keep out of his way. Yelling and screaming, the men on both sides cursed at each other. Many men died and nearly all were Helgs.

"Hold!" A command from the Helgs rang out. A slight pause, then, "Hold I said." The Helg line wavered before falling back into the little space left to them.

The Maxilla, Stormborn and Temujin warriors paused and waited.

An officer appeared in the middle of the Helgs. He had removed his tunic to reveal a flowing shirt of yellow. Long braided hair hung down his back and he gripped a golden sword, a special curved sword. Some of the Maxilla men muttered that he looked like a butterfly with a golden sting.

The eyes exuded warmth but the sword looked cold and sharp. Tarn thought the combination appeared carefree, yet deadly. As he stood before him, the warrior performed a series of short exercises to stretch various muscles.

As Tarn impatiently waited, the moves evoked memories of a bygone meeting. An image of Eral, a master swordsman, flowed into his mind. Students with particular talents were taken from their families at nine years of age to a training camp in Cpin, a small city in the vastness of Turlo. If they survived the rigours of the harsh regime for six years they would be taught the finer arts of the craft, although another five years would elapse before the true synergy between man and sword emerged. They never stopped learning and seldom ceased fighting – premature death being the normal cause.

Some years previously, Eral had approached Tarn in a tavern on the border between Maxilla and Turlo. He was between work and pleasure; bored to distraction. Seeking new employment, Eral asked whether the Bokin Band could use his skills. They had talked, became friendly, even sparred together, but had not grown close. Tarn liked the man but not the mercenary. Their paths had crossed several times since and a friendship had grown. It had been built on mutual respect yet failed to fully blossom. Tarn could never comprehend a man who would sell his skills for money, for work to kill was an ethic he loathed.

As the yellow shirt finally ceased flowing around the lithe body, the warrior threw his golden sword high in the air. The blade flashed like lightning. One slip would remove a finger but he caught the hilt effortlessly before turning and bowing to Tarn.

Tarn's face showed no expression. He knew he faced a formidable opponent for the skills of Cpin men were legendry.

"I am Dravino, and you are?"

"Tarn."

"Ah … yes, my good friend Eral told me about you. A good man, I believe he said. That's if my memory serves me well. Alas, he is no more. A dagger in the back whilst bedding an agile young wench would likely kill anyone. Still, rumour has it that his cries of ecstasy sent him to the gods with a smile on his face."

"I am sorry. A man like that needs to die with a sword in his hand. I respected his talent," Tarn said.

"Yes indeed, but he was never a likeable man. Let us move on to more pressing matters. You hold a broadsword, mine is a scimitar, smaller and lighter. I am the fastest swordsman that has ever lived. This must be a fair contest … do you wish to change swords?"

"No."

"When I defeat you, I may let you live. Of course that depends on how well you fight."

"Then fight," Tarn said.

Tarn approached and the swordsman bowed once more, then invited him to dance as he moved around on light feet. All other fighting gradually ebbed away as men on both sides eagerly awaited the clash. The two swordsmen circled each other, neither wishing to make a move, weighing up the possibilities. Both held their swords in their right hand. Tarn leapt forward then threw himself violently sideways as his opponent switched his blade from right to left. To his horror Tarn faltered and almost lost his footing. An ambidextrous fighter was rare and one to be very wary of. The speed of his opponent's riposte astonished him; the ripped flesh across his chest, a clear warning. A master swordsman stood before Tarn, yet he felt no fear, only hatred. His mind was in killing mode now. He knew that this man would die or he would.

"You move fast, for one uncultured in the finer arts of swordsmanship."

"And you talk too much."

"So be it," Dravino said.

A quick attack, a parry and another cut on Tarn's chest. Dravino attacked again and again. Tarn parried each with difficulty, sending out a riposte as and when he could, but the golden sword moved effortlessly from hand to hand as if by sorcery.

Both gripped cutting and slicing weapons but Dravino held the lighter one. Only the longer blade of Tarn's broadsword maintained the balance as Dravino kept his opponent guessing, seeking an opportunity to strike. The fluid movements mesmerised Tarn. He felt his mind relax. The song of steel and gold echoed inside him as a lullaby of distraction, yet even as it soothed him coldness bit into his heart like a shard of ice. A clarity of thought emerged and forced the berserker to remain dormant. He allowed Dravino to attack, parrying each one, biding his time. He sent no riposte but kept moving, his feet shifting to the commands of his brain. The deadly blades sang their song. Dravino as fast as the wind, swinging his single blade; Tarn constantly blocking with his double-edged weapon. So fast did they move that many could not keep up with the action. Tarn knew that for all his speed, Dravino, being lighter and smaller, was faster, and unlikely to tire first. Against all his normal instincts he watched and waited, saving his strength.

Dravino continued to attack and Tarn blocked. With each parry, Dravino smiled as he pushed Tarn back – but little by little every stroke carried less strength. Tarn observed, yet felt almost detached from the reality of the contest. As the maestro slowed, Tarn could see that he dropped his right shoulder just before he switched his blade from right to left. Eventually an opening presented itself and Tarn instantly reacted.

The shoulder dropped and, as Dravino changed hands, Tarn swept his heavy broadsword down towards his unsuspecting head. With reflexes like a cat, Dravino instantly blocked the killing stroke, but the weight of the impact smashed his magnificent scimitar in half. Tarn's sword carried through, opening a deep cut in his opponent's head. Dravino dropped to one knee with blood freely flowing from the wound. He shook his head as if struggling to focus. Tarn, unrelenting, stood over him with lifeless eyes.

"Finish it."

Tarn's lust to kill grew stronger. His sword rose above his head.

A stillness descended over the throng of the warriors as men on both sides wondered. The silence seemed to last longer than the fight.

"You deserve better. What did he offer you?"

"Wealth, my weakness."

"Many are weak but you fought well and with honour. Myracadonis has seduced you with his promises for had you won, I doubt they would have been kept. You are my captive and I give you my word that no harm will befall you. My doctors will attend to your needs for your skills should not be wasted. There are many who would appreciate your tutelage in the art of swordplay. I claim this sword for my own. It will be re-forged. Does it have a name?"

"Faith."

Tarn's company cheered. But the Helgs backed away, uncertain what to do. Some ran, whilst others unsheathed swords and lashed out at those around them. Tarn's swordsmen returned the compliment. Small battles started anew, growing as more men tried to attack or defend each other. Tarn ordered two guards to escort Dravino from the field of battle, and to take great care with the magnificent sword. As he turned back to his men, a Helg charged at him with a spear held above his head. Tarn ducked underneath and cut the man in two. Another charged, meeting the same fate. His men pressed the Helgs on three sides. Having nowhere to go, the Helgs fought on, and perished.

Tarn could see the remaining Helgs looking backwards with fear in their eyes. Something had to give; one more push, then another, and it was over. The Helg line broke in disarray, running like the wind as the incoming tide swept all before it.

They scurried back to stand under Rope's End Rock and reformed once more, yet looked like a tired and bloody rabble, broken apart by the sheer force of the attackers. The Helg line showed little sign of being able to fight on, let alone win.

Shaking from head to toe, Tarn stood alone in the middle of the battleground, his mind disturbed. He wanted to throw his sword away on seeing so many bodies surrounding him. The slaughter was unimaginable. The dead would stay dead but the whimpers and cries from the wounded tore into him. Searing pain swept through his head as he sank to his knees. His body ached with fatigue, washing over him like the longest sleep of all. He closed his eyes to escape from the bloodshed, seeking an inner peace as bit by bit he willed his mind to function normally. As his senses slowly returned, the monster faded away. Rational once more, he rose, wiping the blood from his face and hands, staring to the north.

"Captain. Captain Tarn, can you hear me," Mellis said.

"Tarn, look at me," Wynne said. "It's over."

"I fear not. Look! This is only the beginning."

Myracadonis had appeared on a ledge above his followers, a golden corona swirling around his black cape. The Horned Demon burned brightly behind him.

CHAPTER 17

"You can't mean that," Lowis said. "It's utter madness."

"It's simple," Grona explained. "We take this trail to the bottom of the gorge and then we ride towards Rope's End Rock. They won't be expecting us to attack from the rear. Think of the surprise on their faces when they see their unexpected visitors."

"Four against hundreds. It's not madness, more like bloody suicide," Terryn said.

"Stupid, but the first rule of a soldier is obedience," Eagle-Eye said mockingly.

Grona ignored the taunt. "As I said before, lads – time to earn your pay. Think of the hero's welcome when we return."

"Think of the long time dead," Terryn said.

"Kill this shaman, enjoy the spoils of war, then ride home as the brave men of Rope's End Rock. Come on lads, what do you say?"

Eagle-Eye had continued to look at the land below. "I see a small rear-guard to the east. Five men, no more. The cover is good for over one hundred paces behind them. We can overcome these few, but what then, Grona?"

"We climb up the track behind the rock and kill the whoreson."

"Why didn't I think of such a ... simple plan," Terryn said.

"Simple plans are my speciality. Saddle up, lads."

"If I die, I am coming back to haunt you ... you old bastard," Terryn said.

"I doubt they let anyone leave Hell," Grona retorted as the others sniggered.

Up until then Eagle-Eye had looked on with disinterest. "When two play, one must die. Your time has come, shaman."

The others listened carefully to their reticent friend for his words perfectly summed up their thoughts.

On returning to their mounts, Jemson had saddled up and was turning his horse around.

Grona grabbed the reins.

"I'm not coming with you," Jemson said.

"You wanted to be a man, now is your chance," Grona said.

Jemson shook his head, savagely pulled the horse's head around and kicked hard. Grona fell to the ground.

"Bollocks," Grona said as Lowis offered a hand up. "I thought he had guts."

"That little shit," Terryn said.

"I never trusted that boy," Lowis said.

"No need to worry. He was so full of fear, it ran right through him," Grona said, pointing to a stinking mess on the ground.

The laughter eased the tension as they mounted, ready to start the descent.

Veterans always knew when to be silent. As the horses cantered down the weedy track Grona's men used the time to think. Terryn longed for the warm body of a whore with big tits and maybe she had a sister. Lowis wanted a big juicy steak cooked rare; Eagle-eye craved a swim in a cool lake. Only Grona thought of what lay ahead. His hands had slipped from the throat of Myracadonis once and he vowed not to let another opportunity pass by.

Compared to the route that Ammett had ridden, this trail ran smooth. They rode as fast as the terrain would allow, yet not too fast, aware that a large cloud of dust could reveal their position. Grona raised his hand as they neared the junction with the gorge. Without any orders Eagle-Eye dismounted and crept forward through the dense foliage, his keen vision missing nothing.

He beckoned to his brothers in arms, index finger on parched lips as they crawled forward. "The guards still look to the west. No other Helg is in sight. There is perfect cover on the far side of this main trail. If we are very careful they will never know what happened … until they awake in Hell."

Grona patted him on the shoulder as a wide grin spread across his face, but it evaporated in a flash when the sounds of charging horses and the battle cries of men filled the air. Grona took decisive action: a point of his hand, a simple finger motion and within minutes all four of them lay hidden on the north side of the gorge. The dense undergrowth gave them confidence, as did their self-belief. In less than ten minutes they could smell sweat with a hint of piss and shit. Eagle-Eye held his nose and Terryn nearly choked as he desperately tried to suppress a laugh that threatened to explode from his throat.

Grona stood sideways behind a broad pine as the Helgs talked and argued. When one large Helg moved to stand before a tree on the other side of the sentry area, Grona's hand came down.

In a flash three Helgs fell to the floor. Razor-sharp knives slit unsuspecting throats. The fourth fell to an axe in his neck; Grona never missed from ten paces. Only the pissing man had time to turn but, before he could raise more than a whisper, Terryn and Lowis threw themselves at him. One grabbed his throat while the other stabbed all the life out of him. They pulled the bodies away from prying eyes and stripped them, rubbing as much blood as possible from their clothes. Although badly fitting, Grona believed that the uniforms could make them pass for Helg warriors from a distance. A few extra minutes could prove the difference between winning and losing.

They could see the area more clearly. Two tracks led upwards. The easy, well-worn route snaked its way around the cliff whilst another led directly up. It would be difficult but not impossible and would save precious minutes. Grona gave the orders, Terryn and Lowis grimaced, and Eagle-Eye started the ascent.

As he contemplated the climb Grona heard the sounds of battle coming ever nearer. The company had clearly moved forward in the gorge as voices carried towards them. Now it was the turn of his small band to enter the fray. Grona had already missed part of the action and he was damned if he was going to miss the final act. He urged them to hurry. Eagle-Eye had made good progress, so one by one the four Bokin Band warriors began the steep climb up to the rear of Rope's End Rock. The sharp stone gave good grip and they pushed on as fast as they could. The stale stink of sweat on their jerkins and trews accompanied them on the ascent. Perspiration dripped into wide-open eyes, the salty drops stinging. Muscles ached with fatigue and hands and knees scraped on unforgiving rock leaving specks of fresh blood in their wake. A dread of being too late coursed through their bodies and drove them upwards as they scrambled on. Holding their fears in check, they cursed the gods, and Grona, for bringing them here; Grona simply cursed everyone.

They expected to meet Helg soldiers as they neared the top but none materialised. Ahead, a flight of stairs had been cut into the rock. They hoped that it signified the end of the climb. They took a firm grip on their weapons as they clambered over the last rock and onto the first step with Eagle-Eye scouting the way.

At the top of the last step his splayed fingers signalled instant compliance. Four weary warriors dropped to the ground to lie on a flat platform of cold grey stone. As they edged their way forward a perfect view of the gorge greeted them. They watched Tarn defeat a Helg champion, then stride forward to rout the Helgs. They looked in wonder at the numerous red and black caves below them, as well as the obscure drawings on stone outcrops. As they took in the winding rocky paths that made access possible they viewed women and children standing at the mouths of the caves watching the action unfold.

With their bodies looking forward and downward it was clear to Grona that no one had seen them arrive and they were invisible from below.

A look of surprise crossed the faces of Grona's small band. All of the Helg warriors appeared to be in the gorge, for as hard as they searched, none could be seen on the paths below.

Seeing Tarn slump to the hard ground, Terryn pointed. Was he injured? A sigh of relief rose from all their lips as he rose once more. As a silence enveloped the battleground they clearly heard Althalos and Wynn speaking. But their hearts fell as they heard Tarn say, "I fear not. Look! This is only the beginning."

Myracadonis stood on a rock below them. The Horned Demon sent dazzling waves of light high into the air. Halos of fire rose and grew ever larger before sending out whips of flame. Skeletons holding flaming lances and riding black horses emerged from the cliffs. Those standing before the shaman cried out in terror.

They saw Wynne pull Tarn backwards, away from the flames. Others followed as the flames sought to devour them. Those too frightened to move, died where they stood.

Lowis and Terryn covered their ears. Ammett curled up in a ball. All of them tried to sink lower into the rock as the noise deafened them. Grona recovered first as the noise abated.

"You won't escape me again. Time for you to pay, your whoreson," Grona said.

Grona made everything seem so simple. All they had to do was to follow the path, descend one level, surprise the shaman, kill him, take the glory and return home as heroes all.

Terryn suggested praying – praying that all eyes would be looking downwards. Lowis agreed, adding that maybe Grona had ridden in the hot sun for too long. Eagle-Eye licked his lips and sent a deadly look in Grona's direction. Grona ignored the comments and the stare for all his energy would be centred on killing the shaman, no matter what it took.

This man-made track, scored deep into the hard rock, was a masterpiece of design. It cut into the contours of the mountainside and was easily wide enough for two men and their horses to travel in safety. Many hand-holds had also been cut to provide safe passage for the women and children. Other tracks, both ascending and descending, allowed access to the differing levels. Grona counted fifteen, including the upper level on which he stood. The task would have taken many years to achieve. They marvelled at the fine work as they walked slowly to the first downward slope, hugging the inner rock for secrecy, yet meeting no one. Below they could see Myracadonis re-energising his troops; a few hundred heavily armed reserves ran from hidden tunnels to bolster their routed comrades.

At the junction, Grona motioned and all of them men drew their swords. Silent as cats they descended the slope, edging ever closer to the burning light. With all eyes turned towards the scene below, the four warriors believed that a surprise attack from the rear could be successful but whatever the cost this shaman must die.

They temporarily lost sight of their quarry as the trail bent inwards. Grinning faces belied their fear but at least now they could move unseen. As they reached the inner curve Grona stopped. He looked at his friends. One by one, he stared deeply into cold unwavering eyes. A brief smile, a nod of his head and they moved. Their destiny awaited them around the next bend. Ten yards, they could hear every word. Five yards, they could feel the heat from the Horned Demon. Two yards and they ran forward.

CHAPTER 18

TARN MOVED AHEAD of his troops, watching the reinforcements scurrying from the caves with disinterest, even though the latecomers looked well armed. Althalos and Wynne moved to stand either side of him. The rest of the company spread out left and right with the ever-faithful bowmen to the front.

"Come down, shaman. Your forces are almost destroyed. Do not sacrifice any more lives in a battle that you cannot win. Show yourself. You cannot hide forever," Tarn said.

As he spoke two warriors moved to stand alongside Myracadonis. Maxilla bowmen immediately notched arrows, then watched and waited for an opportunity. The sighting uphill would be difficult but at this range some were confident of hitting a target with their larger bows.

"You fool, you think me beaten? These … can be replaced. Believers in the Horned Demon are everywhere. My powers grow. Why should I come down?"

Without warning the archers loosed and Myracadonis instinctively jumped back. The two men fell from the rock, screaming in agony until they hit the ground below. The women and children started wailing all over again, but, unfortunately for the company, the shaman reappeared unscathed.

"You are quick off the mark, Tarn, but your arrows cannot harm me. Your forces are too small and too pitiful."

Tarn's face flushed with anger at the man's arrogance. His gaze exuded a wave of hatred for this loathsome creature.

"Let me show you what I mean, here is a small demonstration of my capabilities."

With a wave of the shaman's hand lightning erupted from the Horned Demon. Silver tongues licked at individual bowmen turning them instantly into burning ashes. With over twenty dead some of his troops fell back. Tarn ordered everyone else to do the same.

"This is my fight, and mine alone," he said to his big friend.

"You need me to hold your hand," Wynne replied.

Althalos also stayed. "I must honour my fallen prince and stand with you."

Mellis simply walked forward and stood with his feet apart.

"As you wish," then more softly, "I am proud to stand with my friends."

The shaman held his arms aloft. With a wisp of blue smoke he rose from the rock. His followers, standing by the mouths of caves and on the walkways, kneeled as Myracadonis floated down into the gorge. His soldiers bowed in supplication. As he moved through the air, his black cape billowed behind. The silver stars and hideous faces that covered it sparkling in the sun. A hush descended as he flew like a silent bird of the distant ocean. Myracadonis landed like a spectre, his feet leaving no mark in the dust. An aura of power gathered in energy as the shaman's eyes watched malevolently.

"My magical power is too strong for your brawn. You cannot win. Your warriors will perish. Do you want the sound of wives and children sobbing into the night for the loss of their men? Do you wish to see your terrified people, hiding in castles and villages, falling under my spell? The land will be desolate as I conquer all who oppose me. And know this, Captain Tarn of the Bokin Band – you have been lured into my carefully planned trap. I have only allowed you to see a little of my potency, to tease and inflame you. My strength has grown ten-fold since the last battles, all those years ago. The apprentice has matured and now I will leave my mark on this pathetic world."

"Brave words from a defeated shaman. More warriors are coming. Your power is on the wane. You can fight and die or, as I said before, you can surrender and save more deaths. Make a choice, shaman. I am bored with listening to your prattles."

Mocking laughter filled the air. "Why do you not listen? Why do you not understand? I do so admire your fighting skills and your leadership qualities but this land will be mine. All who resist will never grow old. But for you, there is a way forward, a way for you and your men to survive. Come. Let us be allies. I need a good man to lead my army. You can save your people from further suffering. Protect their future. Come join me, live longer than you could ever envisage and share in riches beyond your imagination."

"Sharing? Pah! You only know how to take. Look at all these people. You have stolen the minds of so many, leaving empty husks and tormented souls behind. Turning farmers and townsfolk into fighters, and innocents into slaves, is the work of the devil. Whilst I breathe, shaman, evil will never conquer this land, for men like me will always rise up and fight, especially against a coward. For all cowards are bullies." Tarn drew his sword and pointed it to the heavens.

"I will never join a murderer and a coward."

The men's cheers soon changed to rage as the insults flew thick and fast.

"You are disappointing, yet so predictable Tarn. I offer you the world and impossibly long life but you choose death. Luckily for you, I am a merciful man for I will not kill you today, nor any day. Death would be too permanent for you need time to reflect on your stupidity, to remember your failure to serve. So perhaps a little trip to the unknown should do. Yes, I see fear in your eyes. That is how it should be. Prepare yourself for a journey you will never forget."

A shockwave of cold ran through Tarn, chilling his body to the core. He tried frantically to move any of his limbs but only a part of his brain still functioned.

Myracadonis sneered as he closed his eyes. His face turned chalky white. Wrinkles and deep furrows appeared all over his body as he aged a hundred years in seconds. The incandescent power of the Horned Demon surged downwards into his body and he began to chant in a strange tongue. Tarn had heard enough. He willed his body to move towards the shaman and finally his limbs decided to obey. As the spell broke, Myracadonis opened his arms to the heavens.

"Peltross haddesun."

Blinding light surged from the shaman's hands, filling Tarn with a shooting pain that ran around his body like a thousand small cuts, each trying to cause the most hurt. His body was lifted from the ground and he desperately tried to hold on to something or anybody. Wynne leapt into the air but missed Tarn's hand by a whisker, singeing his own in the attempt. A cascade of colour, a terrible scream and Tarn vanished. The Horned Demon continued to throb.

Although initially stunned into silence, men surged forward yelling and screaming for revenge. Wynne drew his sword and cut deeply into the shaman's body yet the withered carcass did not react. Wynne was unafraid of anything but this unnerved and terrified him. How could he fight nothing? He had heard stories of such powerful magic but had never believed them. Now all his physical strength was meaningless for he had failed his best friend. He fell to his knees and cursed all the gods.

The shaman's body began to slowly reform. Within a few minutes he stood before them once more, seemingly unaffected by his ordeal.

"What did you say? Where have you sent him, Myracadonis?" The big man demanded answers.

"In your tongue – go to Hell. Tarn now stands before the doors of that evil place. They won't let him in and they won't let him leave. He is destined to be tormented between Heaven and Hell for all eternity."

Maniacal laughter echoed all around the gorge.

differences became apparent. "As the Horned Demon follows the amulet, so it follows Myracadonis, for the amulet alone has no power. He does not need the amulet when the Horned Demon is so close. Yes, the amulet glows brightly here, but the power is travelling along that." He pointed at the luminous beam flowing endlessly into the shaman. "Kill the beam, kill Myracadonis."

"Easier said than done, my friend," Lowis said.

"Well, this will do for a start." Grona threw the amulet onto the ground and stamped on it. A rumble of grief made them look up; the beam trembled in flight, slightly deviating from its course. Grona looked at the amulet on the ground before smashing it into small pieces with the hilt of his sword. "Now what do you make of that, you bastard?"

The Horned Demon groaned in pain. The colours briefly changed from red to black and then back to red, the beam quivering.

"That's it," Grona shouted, deafening his men. "This symbol feels sorrow, it feels pain; it may not be human but if it can feel then it can be hurt or destroyed. Myracadonis has no power without it."

Eagle-Eye moved as close as he could to the Horned Demon. "It really is a hideous bastard. I have a small hunting bow. Maybe an arrow would affect the light, or at least cause a little damage."

"Why not piss in the wind," Terryn said. "Ok! Ok! Anything is worth a try."

The arrow disappeared into the fiery heart.

"What now?" Terryn said.

The men questioned him but drew no response. They pulled him away from the edge but still he stared into space, so Terryn slapped him hard across the face.

"Wake up, you old bastard. What do we do?"

The spell broke, leaving one angry Grona.

"Do that again, Terryn, and I will cut your throat and feed your entrails to the pigs."

"So glad you are back to your normal loving self," Terryn said. The words belied his concern for, in all the years that he had known Grona, complete inaction from the old warrior was unheard of.

Grona stood up and walked to stand under the image of the Horned Demon. "That is the cause. That is the canker. It must be removed."

"How do you know?" his men asked.

"I don't know for sure, but why this?"

He opened his hand. The amulet shone brightly, the rays growing stronger. Moving farther from the Horned Demon caused the light to dim.

"This draws power from that bloody demon."

"You mean that the closer the amulet is to the light the more powerful it becomes. No wonder the shaman needed to be close to the Horned Demon," Lowis said.

Terryn rubbed a lump of dirt from his face. "But why would he not wear it now? It makes no sense."

Grona looked again at the amulet, seeking answers. He watched sunbursts radiate as he moved around the wide platform. Subtle table and two chairs sat in the middle of a dismal cave, with a smaller table and chair against the side wall. Thick blankets, woven with an image of the Horned Demon, hung from the walls. A big wooden cot, probably his bed, stood in one corner. Numerous books lay in random piles across the floor whilst unusual artefacts of silver and bronze nestled in an alcove. One statue of a helmeted warrior holding a skull caught Grona's gaze. The red eyes sent out a dull luminosity as he picked it up but a sharp pain ended his interest. He wanted to examine the bronze man more closely but they had to move fast. It would take a week to investigate the rest of the cave, so Grona called a stop. They had to go. As he left, his eyes were drawn to an amulet sitting in the middle of the small table. It throbbed with a yellow glow as he approached. On picking it up, rays of orange and gold shone forth and a small sun lit up the cave. His men marvelled at the light but Grona stuck it in his pocket. The rest of the cave could be explored later, but for now more pressing matters required his attention.

Two minutes later, the small band stood once again to look down on the gorge and saw the shaman chanting.

"Peltross haddesun."

Initially shocked into silence, they shouted and screamed as Tarn disappeared. A stab of conscience hit Grona in the heart. He slumped on the rock ledge, dangling his weary legs over the side. For the second time in his life he felt totally helpless, his mind a whirl of confusing thoughts.

CHAPTER 19

GRONA AND HIS men rounded the corner, but the platform lay empty before them. They had arrived too late, for Myracadonis had already flown downwards and now stood before Tarn and his company. Now that the last rock face lay behind them, every word carried. They could feel the power of the Horned Demon and were forced to shelter their eyes from the dazzling light surging into the body of Myracadonis. The heat of the beam was prodigious.

Searching each other's faces confirmed their own suspicions. Tarn and his men would most likely have to deal with the shaman on their own.

Grona felt a twinge of pride as Tarn refused the offer from Myracadonis, but the feeling quickly passed. His brain required action, his whole body yearned to stand before this foul shaman – to cut the head from the body with one swing of his sword. He wanted that pleasure but what could he do from here? Was there a way down from this lofty perch, he mused?

Eagle-Eye and Terryn frantically searched to the right whilst Lowis joined Grona to the left. A narrow hidden passage led upwards but it only revealed the shaman's living quarters. One large

"Can we climb up to the Horned Demon? Is there a way? Perhaps if we get closer?" Eagle-Eye said.

"Eagle-Eye is right. We must climb the rock," Grona said.

Eagle-Eye delved into his pack and pulled out a sharp axe and a rope.

Grona eyed the rope doubtfully. "Will it hold?"

"Yes … hopefully," Eagle-Eye said under his breath.

"Then give me the rope."

"I am the better climber, I should go," Lowis said.

"You climb like a three legged goat," Terryn retorted.

"Damn you both. Give me the bloody rope." With Grona's face inches from theirs, both men backed away.

With the rope securely tied to his midriff, Grona climbed very carefully. His huge strength allowed him to hold on to the cracks in the rock but Grona would never be known for his nimbleness.

Progress slowed to a stop as he neared a smooth section. He forced the axe deeply into a crevice then tied one end of the rope to the handle. Hammering in the axe with the hilt of his dagger secured the bond.

He briefly checked the tightness of the rope around his waist, then swung. His men watched, awaiting the fall, but unknown to them Grona could see the way upwards, no more than an arm span away. The rope held. His hands immediately found a grip and his feet secured a good foothold. Ignoring the cries of encouragement from below, he made the climb look easy. The luminosity was amazing, forcing him to move one hand to shield his eyes. The Horned Demon delivered a constant stream of light towards the shaman who appeared to have grown in stature. Grona looked at the scene below – the uncertainty, the loss of hope, all written across the faces of Tarn's assembled company.

He thought of his life, his men and his promise.

"Here I come, you whoreson."

He dived directly into the heart of all his anger.

~~~

With an explosion, the rainbow colours disappeared and the sky darkened. Grona's men dived for cover as cascades of burning rock burst into the air. The rocks tried hard to defy gravity but what goes up must come down.

Eagle-Eye had survived without a scratch whereas Terryn and Lowis had been hit by a hurricane of sharp stones. But lady luck had waved her magic wand, for if they had been standing anywhere other than directly underneath the Horned Demon their demise would have been instantaneous. As Eagle-Eye would remind them later: you fly like a hawk, you bleed when you land. Although bruised, cut and bloodied, they survived, astonished that the blast had not swept them off the rock ledge.

Those in the gorge had a little more time to react, but numerous died – especially the Helg reinforcements closest to the rock face. Grona's comrades viewed the scene below, seeking out friends, helpless to assist yet concerned for all the company. As men slowly pulled themselves out of shock, the screams of the wounded echoed from one side of the gorge to the other. They could see the unaffected Helgs standing in silence, unable to fully comprehend now that the pull of the Horned Demon had vanished.

Their minds appeared to flow as freely as a child's dream as they wandered about, but they were neither awake nor asleep. In limbo, they stood and stared into the distance. Those on the walkways and ledges had thrown themselves flat yet none had been injured for rocks had fallen into the middle of the gorge. Only a couple of children received cuts and grazes as their mothers had pushed them to the ground and protected them with their own bodies.

From their rock platform they saw Wynne pull himself upright from a pile of rubble, and a dusty Althalos rising on wobbly legs to stand alongside him. The two men could be heard issuing orders, trying to unravel the disorder.

Grona's men tried to clear the deafness from their heads, hoping that it would be temporary. With such a loud explosion, they could see many friends holding their hands over their ears, whilst others tried to stem the blood running from ruined eyes. Yet Tarn's company had fared far better than the enemy. Ears previously impaired, listened to the sounds of death and destruction whilst closed eyes opened to view the scene of chaos. Shaking off the dust and fear, the company moved quickly to disarm and then help their bewildered foes.

Crying women began to descend from their caves, bringing water and clean rags. Although stunned they were less affected than their men folk and moved as quickly as they could. Some held hands, others hugged children, whilst two old crones skilled in herbs and medicines carried tinctures and ointments. They joined with the company healers, moving towards those that could be saved. Men sought comrades in the desperate hope that they had survived. Some vomited at the sight of the badly charred corpses. Others covered their faces, whilst some chased away a flock of crows casually waiting their turn for the forthcoming banquet. Order slowly returned; the road back to normality had begun. It would be a long one.

Wynne looked at the debris of rocks and bodies, his eyes constantly searching. Seeing Grona's men yelling and waving he returned the wave, but not the cheers. He saw Terryn and Lowis exchange glances; they know what I seek, he thought.

The big warrior placed a thick cloth over his nose as he turned over the bodies. The force of the explosion had charred many Helgs beyond recognition, propelling some body parts forward to cover those still alive. Undeterred, Wynne continued his search. Wynne saw the glint of silver beneath a corpse and a pile of burnt clothing.

Heaving the remains aside revealed a comatose figure wrapped in a black cloak. Wynne pulled the man to his feet.

He could hear Grona's men shouting as loudly as they could. "Kill the bastard. Boil him in oil." Those below took up the shouts, crowding around as close as possible. All in the gorge heard Wynne's voice as it echoed from rock to rock.

"Hide from me, would you? I think not."

Myracadonis said nothing.

"I made a promise. Do you remember? Did you hear it?"

"Nooo," the shaman squealed. Wynne saw him coughing out the dust that must have caked his mouth.

"Found your voice have you? You sent boys, *children* to do your work. They fought and died in your name. Murderer!"

"I swear … it was the Horned Demon, not me. It controlled me. I didn't know what I was doing."

"I see fear has brought back your wits but a silver tongue will not save you shaman. For years you have pitted tribe against tribe. Thousands died. Babes in arms, women, the old and the weak, all have perished in your name. And look at these people; the Helgs have been corrupted beyond any imagination. You have feasted on the strength of nations for too long. Why should I spare you?"

He viewed the face of Myracadonis as it searched for any assistance. But Wynne knew that only faces of stone stared back.

"You are a simple man with simple tastes, Wynne of Lakeside. If you had visited me all those years ago, I could have saved your Gisella. You had your chance then; now you have another. Save me and I may be able to bring her back."

The soothing words stabbed like a knife into Wynne's heart. He staggered as images of his beloved dying in his arms appeared before his eyes. Memories of Gisella blurred as he remembered a man who spoke dangerously, promising to cure Gisella with a potion, yet hinting that he required something in return. He had questioned him yet received no clear answers. Cold eyes had glinted with malice, a sneering face with arrogance. Wynne saw that face clearly inside his head. This could not be the same man.

"You bastard! How could it be? Everything about you is different, even your eyes. You lie … shaman."

"As my power has grown, so has my appearance. I liked little about my previous form so why should I not alter? It took many years for the change to be complete, but here I am, ready to help, as I offered those years past. I can assist you all on the road to recovery. I can assuage your hurts. Both sides have lost many; we have all suffered. This has all been a terrible misunderstanding. Come, let us all be friends and put the past behind us. What do you say?"

The soft voice cajoled them, mesmerising in its gentleness, lulling some within earshot to nod their heads in agreement. A murmur spread through the front ranks.

"Stop!" Wynne yelled. "You have no power."

"In a short time, it will return. Trust me."

Wynne took a step backwards, breathing heavily as fresh blood flushed out old wounds. He remembered similar words from the last time they met. A perfect image of his beloved formed inside his head, her smile shining like a golden sun, and Wynne knew that the spell had been broken.

He stepped forward, blade in hand. A fire burned in his belly sending a clear message. It was time to act. He drew the weapon back and put all of his anguish, all of his love, behind the stroke that would end the shaman's evil forever. The torso of Myracadonis toppled over and his head landed to spin on the ground several feet away.

"Not this time, shaman." Wynne turned to the men. "I vowed to you all that I would kill this … thing. No longer will his magic destroy lives. I honour my best friend. My day is done."

As the men cheered he started to walk away.

"Burn the body and head immediately. Scatter the ashes to the four winds," he ordered.

CHAPTER 20

INTENSE LIGHT OVERPOWERED his senses. His body burned hot as flames licked at his face. Tarn lost all sense of time as his muscular frame swirled round and round in a frenzy of malice. Sharp, quick stabbing pain ran from head to toe and back again, as if a thousand birds constantly pecked him. Deathly faces covered in blood and gore surrounded him. A constant moaning assaulted his ears. Any coherent thought eluded him as fear and hurt ruled his mind. Lost in a demonic tornado, Tarn's body and soul wilted in the wind.

As consciousness returned he awoke on his back at the base of a small hill, stinking like a muddy wallow, his breathing ragged. Trying to stand caused his legs to give way so he pulled his knees together and adopted a foetal position. The ground looked firm enough but on closer inspection he saw that his eyesight had deceived him. If he pushed hard, his hands sank into a primeval ooze. The liquid cleared before changing back to the consistency of mud. Dead people floated just below the surface; those facing upwards opened their eyes as they passed, staring accusingly at Tarn. Small creatures attacked anything that moved. A stream of green weed passed, changing shape, leaving red spots in its wake. Frogs jumped in and out of the mire, resurfacing with strips of bloody meat hanging from open mouths.

A young woman with long grey hair passed underneath him. He watched her intently, unable to take his eyes off the small fish leaving a trail of blood as they nibbled at her naked body.

Dull vacant eyes opened. "Leave this place. There must be a way. The road is hard but you are strong."

"I can dig you out."

"No! Sink into the swamp and here you will remain for all eternity. Torture is favoured by the demons. Go!"

Her eyes closed as she drifted away on an underwater current.

On looking around Tarn noticed a number of mottled patches where no water or swamp swept below. Deciding to take a chance he stood up, then placed a foot on a likely spot. The ground proved to be firm. A sigh escaped from tight lips. With both feet now on solid earth he looked around, and saw the dark battling with the light for superiority over the hills and scorched grasslands. Violet and red lightning flashes attacked the land in a never-ending salvo.

Torrential rain flooded the hollows but quickly evaporated as a new sun burnt the land dry. Wind grumbled like a hungry bear, seeking to devour anything that dared to challenge its might.

"What a hellish place," he said out loud.

"So true." The voice came from behind him.

Tarn drew his sword and swung around, surprising himself with his speed of movement. The largest crow he had ever seen sat on a fence post nearby, its black beak huge and deadly, eyes all seeing.

"It never fails to amaze me how quickly powers return. Being young and brave help, of course, but then others would say that the foolish brave perish quickly."

Relaxing slightly, Tarn sheathed his sword.

"What are you talking about, old bird."

The crow chuckled. "Old is true, chatterbox I am, but you're the one between Heaven and Hell. You can listen or you can leave. All roads end up somewhere. But which one will you choose?"

"Which one would you choose?"

Another chuckle. "Everyone asks that question. You know the answer. Can't you ask something more ... original?"

Running fingers through his filthy hair only made the smell worse, so Tarn stopped and thought before replying. "Clearly I have a choice. You are my ... guide?" The bird nodded. "Then you cannot tell me but you can show me?"

"Not quite, but you're getting warmer. I do love this little game. It keeps my ancient mind active. So how about another question?"

The place reeked of evil. Tarn could taste it in the air and feel it through his boots. The crow told him that he was between Heaven and Hell, so if he made the right choice ...

"Can demons be killed?"

"With your sword and with luck, yes."

"So can you take me to one?"

The crow nearly fell off its perch. "An original question at last. Stupid, but original. Why?"

"Choosing the right path."

"Clever. Very clever, but I doubt you will ultimately triumph for the odds are stacked against you. One demon leads to others; they hunt in packs, tormenting the steady supply of new souls. Do you think that you can conquer them all?"

Tarn ignored the question. "Show me the way."

A flap of huge wings and the bird lifted silently into the air, drifting on an eddy of blue. Tarn followed slowly, wary of the ground beneath. Gripping his sword tighter gave him a sense of security in this world of suffering, but his self-belief never wavered for if the demon could be killed then he would do it. The thought of leaving this world of evil drove him forward. He would depart or die in the attempt.

The hill, so close, wavered in the distance like a mirage. Although he followed the crow towards it, the gap did not appear to narrow. Time passed slowly. He felt like one of the walking dead. Forcing the nagging doubt from his mind, Tarn concentrated on placing one foot in front of the other. Eventually a fence emerged from the murk. The path led through a gap before meandering on towards a distant hill. The crow settled on a fence post, tucking his cumbersome wings under his body.

Tarn stretched his aching legs. "That ... was a long walk." The crow ignored him, having more important matters to attend to.

"I hate these wings," he said, still trying to adjust them. "Now, what do you see?"

"You, old bird, a hill, track and a fence."

"You are one of the few that can make me laugh." The crow flew to the post on the other side of the gap still testy with his feathers. "Clearly you still trust your eyes."

A frown, followed by a wide-open mouth, greeted the crow.

"There is no gate."

"Wonderful; you are indeed a clever warrior, Tarn. It simply takes you a little while to show it."

"You know my name?"

"I take back the clever comment."

"But there is no ... " Tarn stopped in mid flow. There had to be a gate. He looked harder.

"As you believe, so it will happen."

A rotten four-bar gate appeared, swinging on squeaky hinges. A small creature sat astride the gate and glared at him through luminous yellow eyes. It bared sharp teeth and jumped towards him, growing in statue until they met eye to eye. Saliva dripped from long fangs eager to feed and talons caked in blood hung from hairy arms. The deathly gaze bored through Tarn as if seeking to drain his life-force.

With a swing of his broadsword the head fell from wide shoulders. A viscous liquid, blue and black squirted from the head. An eerie scream resonated as the torso floated away on a stinking current.

"It has sent the call for help. More demons will come. What now, my fearless friend?"

"I will follow the trail upwards. Whatever comes my way, I will kill it."

Ever logical, Tarn thought. The words tumbled out but inside his stomach churned. He rubbed his eyes as once again doubts entered into his head. His worst nightmares had never been as bad as this. The unimaginable had been thrown together in a pot to create a mixture of churning chaos, a vile dish to be served to those souls destined to stand in the abyss.

His mind faltered but something deep inside urged him to overcome his fears. There had to be a way and he would find it.

He concentrated on the bird for this uncannily human crow knew more than he had disclosed. The knowledge would be invaluable, if he could only find a way to extract the information.

"You know my name. What is yours?"

"I have many names – The Crow of Despair, Darkside and others. Many, like you, have called me Old Bird. I accept them all, but in reality I am the Gatekeeper between the two spiritual worlds. Heaven is one way, Hell the other."

"As the gatekeeper you have responsibilities. What are they?"

"You ask the questions, etcetera … and I do my best. Standing in between, I see many lost souls."

"Is my fate pre-determined?"

"A good question, and I would answer yes and no. Yes it has but it can be changed."

"Do not play mind tricks on me, old bird. Explain."

"Your doom is to remain between the two gates of good and evil forever. But here time stands still, so what constitutes a period of time in your world means nothing here. You can determine your own fate for a while, but I must warn you – the weak-minded fall into the mire quickly. Those of strong will like you fall more slowly, yet the depth of despair will always creep insidiously into the mind, gnawing at the essence of a soul. Eventually all succumb. There is no escape."

"Confusing words again, old bird. Did you not say that my fate could be changed?"

"Indeed, but unlikely."

"You test my patience, crow."

"You cannot leave here without outside help."

Tarn looked at the bird. His mind was in turmoil, and his broad shoulders sagged into their sockets. He stood motionless, despondent, looking at the bedlam surrounding him.

"I see you have noticed the disharmony. Calm we are, but away from us the violence and disorder never ceases."

Tarn fought for control of his mind. "I can see with my own eyes, damn you."

"Then you have much to think about and little time."

"Gatekeeper, where does the track lead on the other side of the gate?"

"Which gate, my young warrior?"

Another one exactly like the first had appeared, sitting side by side with the former. Even the ongoing track and the distant hill looked the same.

"By all the gods, this place confuses at every turn," Tarn shouted.

"It is meant to," the Gatekeeper said. "One trail leads to the gates of Hell, the other to Heaven. You must decide – and be quick about it – as the demons will soon arrive. Once your choice is made you cannot return here."

Tarn barely hesitated before pointing at the original gate.

"A wise choice, my young friend. But remember, you are only delaying the inevitable."

"What is on the summit of the hill, old bird?"

"A large cross sits atop the hill. It is the gateway to heaven, but the guardians will not let you near even if you beat the demons."

"Is the cross the key to the door?"

"Perhaps, but only the guardians can answer that question."

"Then I must ask them," Tarn said.

"In that case, my job is finished. I wish you well. But one last piece of advice. Do not leave the track, but beware the track itself. It is not all that it seems."

"Do you give advice to everyone, Gatekeeper?"

"You do not belong here."

The crow rose and spread its mighty wings. A few steady beats and it disappeared into the murk.

The gatekeeper's words hit home as Tarn pushed the gate fully open. The more he focused the clearer he saw. Solid earth covered deep holes.

Hard rock as ancient as time hid pits of emptiness, and green tussocks faded to dust before his eyes. Only the mud appeared to be able to support his weight and that stuck like glue to his feet. But that was the way, for the obvious route led to oblivion.

Tarn commenced the long upward trek. With the light constantly changing and with eyes bulging from their sockets, weary legs begged his brain to cease moving. A terrible fate awaited him but willpower forced him on.

After walking for an age, his jerkin and trews had surrendered to the brown filth, and his knees and elbows pleaded for relief after so many falls and slides.

But at least he lived, he told himself. The top of the hill loomed closer; he estimated another fifteen minutes of toil although the poor visibility prevented him from gauging any distance accurately.

A pool of bright water shimmered under a violet moon. Another path, virginal and empty, appeared to his left, the route circuitous but leading to the top. He ignored them, giving both a wide berth. His chest began to heave with exhaustion as he neared the summit. Each step sent a clear message to his brain.

A large snail left a sea of slime as it glided by, leaving him in its wake. A diamond-backed snake coiled around his leg, causing a stumble. Thoughts of Tasmina failed to reveal an image of her face and he forgot the name of his daughter, yet still he moved, drawing on all of his energy reserves. He could see the top of the hill and a plain iron cross.

A few more paces and all he had to do was reach out and touch it.

A thunderous storm suddenly hit the hillside. Mud and stone turned to a syrup that threatened to wash him away as it oozed and swept downwards. Feet slipped, his face hit the gunge and it took all of his remaining strength to pull himself upright.

A four-armed demon sat on the cross. Two others stood on either side. The leader held a burning sword above his head, the slim blade tapered to a fine point. He held a skull with eyes still intact and open in his other hand. Scaly black tails cracked like thunder. The trio started chanting and a grey mist crept towards Tarn as they exhaled. Two heavy axes appeared in waiting hands as three sets of toxic eyes burnt into his head. Tarn screamed; he had nowhere to go and no more to give. With the demons advancing, Tarn slipped backwards into the mud and awaited the killing blow.

CHAPTER 21

GRONA TRIED TO rub away the flames of blue and green that licked over him, scorching his beard and face. As the initial shock sent a wave of agony through his broad chest he struggled to breathe. Flying through a blackness dotted with tints of colour did little to dissuade him that a meeting with the gods awaited him at journey's end. But which gods, he pondered, as he gripped the hilt of his sword.

He landed in a world of searing heat and pain. Rain fell, swamps formed and screaming rent the air. A bat flew close to his head, baring huge fangs, and he tried unsuccessfully to swat it away. A small dog wagged its wiry tail and tried to take a lump out of his leg. Its protruding canine teeth dripped with gore. When it attacked again, Grona turned and kicked it under the chin. Creatures of all shapes moved around him, some dashing forward with jaws open. Thunder crashed and lightning flickering as the blasts scarred the land in an orgy of destruction.

Ahead he saw three huge demons advance on a fallen shape briefly illuminated against the dark background, their fangs dripping. They began to paw over the bundle of rags which instantly screamed with pain. Leathery black skin gleamed in the light as the bodies writhed to the sound of incessant screeching.

Without hesitation Grona pulled his sword from the scabbard and advanced.

A demon stepped forward swinging a double bladed axe. Stepping neatly inside, he blocked with his sword and punched the creature full in the face. Soft tissue spread like butter; fangs dropped to the ground as the howls of pain started. He dragged his dagger from its leather pouch and plunged it into the exposed neck. Dark goo spread out from the body as it fell, but Grona had already moved on. The second wavered, whilst the leader bent down to the bundle, talons extended.

Grona knew only one way to fight. He swung his broadsword at the creature's head. Black tail swinging, the demon reared backwards just in time. With the body in retreat the scaly tail lashed forward and sent a ripple of needles into Grona's arm. The demon received a grim smile and a deep cut from Grona's dagger in reply. Warily the demon waited, black smoke spewing from mouth and cut. Grona ploughed on regardless even though the four-armed fiend had moved away from probing the shape on the ground. A mighty sword in strong hands could easily remove a man's arm at the shoulder in one stroke.

Grona had already proved to himself that the tough sinew and hardened flesh of a demon was likewise unable to withstand a sustained onslaught. The second demon fell, cut in two by a vicious double-handed stroke.

Ever alert, Grona dived to his right. He felt the swish of a blade in the space where his head had been. Four arms held two swords and two small knives.

"Sneaky bastard – you nearly had me." He rose from the ground, eyes never wavering from the beast.

"Father?" The bundle of rags had spoken.

Stopping a broadsword in mid swing nearly took his right arm from its socket.

"What the …?"

The monster attacked before Grona could finish. Blades nicked his arms and legs and a shallow cut appeared across his chest. Blocking thrust and cut from four different directions almost made him go cross-eyed. He quickly realised that any prolonged defensive action would end badly, so he smirked and beckoned the creature forward. As the scaly monster paused, Grona charged, grasping his sword in his right hand, his dagger in the other. The surprised demon lurched backwards and fought to keep the huge blade away. Grona removed the outer arms with two swift slicing movements. As the man moved relentlessly forward the eyes of the demon watched in horror yet still its slender blade rose in anger, writhing like a deadly serpent on fire. It flickered out with tremendous speed, burning Grona's jerkin. He rubbed the flame away with his knife hand, searing several fingers in the process, but recovered sufficiently to counter the next thrust. The other sword flashed, missing his chest by inches. The demon swung his blades right then left, leaving fire trails in their wake – but Grona kept pressing.

On the downward stroke of the demon's left blade, Grona charged in, ducked under the swinging right sword and stuck his dagger into the nearest eye. Evil black gunge splattered his garments. The screeching was unbearable and he had to cover his ears with both hands. He returned the dagger to its pouch then brushed away the remnants of the fire still smouldering on his jerkin. The continuing howl of the beast drove him mad so he thrust his sword deep into the stomach and out the back. A gurgle and it was over. Removing his sword proved difficult; he had to put his foot on the demon's chest before wrenching it free. He half-expected it to be ruined.

Turning to the bundle on the ground he lifted his son into a sitting position and emptied the contents of his water bottle down a dry mouth.

"So that's what happened to you," he said.

Tarn struggled to speak as the liquid burned in his throat. "What … was that?"

"Does it matter? It worked."

"Leave … we must leave … now."

"How?"

Tarn pointed but his father did not comprehend.

With the little strength that he had left, Tarn grabbed his father's arm, forcing it straight. The murky outline of the iron cross emerged.

Picking Tarn up in his arms, Grona could not believe how light he was. The skin crackled to his touch. Fearing he may cause injury, Grona softened his grip as he walked towards the cross. He looked into his son's face but Tarn had closed his eyes. On reaching his goal Grona waited for a sign, searching for anything or anyone who could return them to their own land. But all he saw was a pack of grey rats attacking the dead bodies of the demons in this hellish land of pain and death. The wind stiffened, blowing strongly upwards from the track. A quiet moan rapidly increased into a loud crescendo of noise.

A black crow arrived to sit on top of the cross, causing Grona to sweep his arm out.

"Stop! This ... this is the Gatekeeper," Tarn muttered.

The swinging arm fell short.

The crow cawed in delight. "I am so pleased to see you, young warrior. Yes, very pleased indeed. Maybe the angels will relent, maybe not, but it is time for you to try – with your father, of course."

"My father ... has saved me ... but I want another saved. The girl in the swamp, she is brave and should not be here."

The wily old bird rubbed its beak on the iron. "Princess Siselle, you mean. The law of the gods is simple – a life for a life, no more, no less. Her life or yours, the choice is clear. But Father Grona, he can offer a life."

"Whose?" Grona demanded.

"Who else? Myracadonis, of course."

"I sense there is more crow, why do you say – of course?"

The crow laughed. "Father Grona, you are as clever as your son. Many want to punish Myracadonis, especially the god of war. Hell awaits him but there are many others here who wish to settle old scores. I know it's not my job, but I can bend most of the rules, so let me simply say that I promised them first bite."

"I did not kill him."

"As good as," the Crow said. "He lost all his power when you launched yourself into the Horned Demon. He will be here soon enough. So, Father Grona, do you offer this gift to the gods, the shaman Myracadonis in exchange for the place of Princess Siselle? I need your acceptance and quickly for other devils are coming."

"I accept." Grona responded immediately. He had no feelings about an unknown girl. His sole desire was to leave this place of horrors as quickly as possible.

"Good, then we have a bargain. The Princess can join the Gods of Light or you can return her to her homeworld. As ever, the choice is yours."

"What did she … do?" Tarn asked, breathless.

"She cut her husband's throat whilst he slept."

"Did he deserve to die?"

"Who is to say, young Tarn. He beat her mercilessly but she had been unfaithful. Life and death are never simple."

"Will the true gods judge her fairly?"

"Naturally, or I would not have offered the choice."

"Then she should be given the chance to join the gods in heaven," Tarn said.

The crow opened its mighty beak and fluffed up its plumage. "It will be as you say, young warrior."

"So be it. I am tired beyond belief, old bird … how can me … and my father return?"

"Simply hold hands and touch the cross. The guardians have made their decision. You can pass."

"But I have not offered a life," Tarn said.

"Quite right, but remember you have received outside help."

"My thanks, Gatekeeper," Tarn said.

Grona scowled. "Mine too … Crow."

"Go now. You do not belong here."

The crow flapped its large wings and lifted into the air. Laughter resonated as it flew away down the trail.

Father and son gripped hands for the first time in over twenty years. Tarn grinned. Grona grimaced before gripping his son's shoulder with his free hand. A flash of amusement tinged with sadness spread across his weather-beaten face as he stood with his son in his arms. As soon as their hands touched the iron cross they vanished, leaving only desolation and the fury of the wind behind.

CHAPTER 22

LATER THAT DAY, Lord Bokin arrived at the gorge with over five hundred horsemen and immediately took command. All of the weary company could rest in peace, refill their bellies and wash away the grime and blood of the battle. Cheers of joy and relief departed dry throats and lips.

"I salute all of you and I grieve for the fallen. We have lost friends, many are injured but all will be remembered for their glorious victory. To learn that Tarn has perished at the hands of the shaman and that Grona has vanished, is a sad day for the Maxilla clan. And we must never forget the sacrifice made by Prince Wren and the Stormborn. Their outstanding valour has saved many lives. I would also like to thank the Temujin for their skill and for supplying so many fine horses."

Lord Bokin breathed deeply, his stomach churning over the loss of so many good men. He wavered over his thoughts, wondering whether he could put into words the feelings that were in his heart.

"I am so proud of all of you. No, I am more than proud. Believe me your actions have saved our nations. You walked into a cunning trap, and against all the odds, you triumphed. I truly believe that Myracadonis's plan was to subjugate all of our people under his evil rule, and he nearly succeeded."

The men stood silently, realising the implications of his words. Lord Bokin raised his right arm.

"I salute the brave men before me and all those now resting with the gods."

Those capable, returned his salute. Some waved, whilst others bowed their heads.

He searched the faces surrounding him, noting their eagerness for news. All wanting answers to the same questions.

"I know that you are wondering about home. Let me be clear. Your families are safe. Some Helgs took the opportunity to ride into our lands for pillage and murder. They failed." Deep frowns changed to happy smiles in an instant. The men cheered loudly, the noise sending the crows flying from their perches in the gorge.

With a wave of his hand, Bokin continued.

"King Leofrick and I amassed fast and light cavalry troops of both Stormborn and Maxilla along our northern borders. Knowing that we would be busy elsewhere, some Helgs decided to act, unwisely as it turned out. Small bands travelled from afar to raid the outlying villages of both nations. The King and I, together with your brothers in arms defeated them. Most of the enemy never returned to their homeland."

The shouts and yells increased in volume. Men threw jugs and hats into the air. A few of the slimmer warriors found that they could defy gravity. Battle hardened soldiers embraced each other, comforted by the knowledge that their families and were safe and proud of their comrade's success.

Another raised hand, an order, and eventually Lord Bokin had the company's attention. "I have left the best to last. No man – not one – was lost. Some were injured but all live, thanks to the gods." Roosting birds flew from the cliff tops, unable to compete with the noise. The men danced, sang and gave thanks. As two barrels of Maxilla's finest red wine appeared the euphoria reached new heights.

Now that he had delivered his message to the men, Lord Bokin turned his attention to other matters. As the shaman had been defeated he ordered that riders be sent with the good news. King Leofrick could stand his men down from the borders and lead them home. A surge of pride ran through Bokin's body as he viewed the tired and happy company before him. He stepped down from a rock to walk amongst them. As he passed by, men carried on cheering, some shed tears; all were happy to be alive. Asking questions, sharing jokes, he tried to speak with as many as possible. Lord Bokin took his time, showing them that he cared.

With the sheer number of the new arrivals now assisting in restoring order to the site of so much bloodshed, the survivors gathered into small groups.

Several doctors had arrived and immediately joined the company healers in their efforts to save as many lives as possible. Alas too many would never see the sun rise again as the loss of blood could not be stemmed quickly enough, even by cauterisation. Infection had also taken its toll on those with previous injuries. Many would be unable to walk on both legs or swing a sword in the future. As the grisly business of counting bodies and naming them began, the ribald laughter at one end of the gorge seemed at odds with the muted sounds elsewhere. Grona's men had descended and followed their comrades to the supply officer. Ale quickly disappeared down men's dry throats.

The joy of being alive drowned their sorrow for the fallen. The name of Grona had already been toasted several times.

Mellis and Althalos had briefed Lord Bokin. They had to repeat some parts of the battle in the gorge as they viewed it from different perspectives and Bokin demanded all the facts. Wynne had drifted away and those ordered to find him had conveniently failed.

"It is a severe loss to learn that Tarn and Grona have fallen. Both had their followers but, apart or together, they were formidable. On our return, we shall honour them. In the meantime, I am proud of you and your men, Mellis. Althalos, the Stormborn have my everlasting thanks. We will return the body of Prince Wren to his kin, with full battle honours. The Maxilla people will never forget."

"Thank you, my Lord," Althalos said.

Mellis pointed towards a nearby group of warrior Helgs. "This place reeks of evil, my Lord, as if madness resides here awaiting to corrupt those who stay too long. Look at them now, lost in a cloud of uncertainty. Some of them still see through misty eyes."

"Will this sickness end? Is it curable?"

"Who could possibly know, my Lord?"

The light had begun to fade and day would turn to night in a few hours. Lord Bokin gave orders for a departure three hours after sunrise the next day.

A single lightning bolt hit a large flat rock illuminating the shadows. Men cursed, shaking fists to the heavens, for the last thing they needed was a soaking.

"By all the gods, it's good to return." Grona's voice sang out as he stood like a colossus on the rock, holding Tarn's lifeless body in his arms. "Now … will someone get me a flagon of ale?"

After the company had surged around Grona and carried him aloft in a large circle, he gave his report to Lord Bokin. The tale amazed him so much that Grona was forced to repeat himself. Stories of the underworld had been told for centuries, mainly to scare naughty children, yet two men, two of his men, had stood before the gates of Hell and survived.

Tarn had recovered enough of his senses to confirm his part, although he admitted there were numerous gaps in his memory. Now resting under a tent, he had succumbed to a deep sleep, courtesy of an opiate.

Lord Bokin had ordered that the fallen be honoured. At the west end of the gorge, a leafy hollow nestled between rings of stone. The dead – Maxilla, Stormborn and Temujin – had been reverently laid to rest. With too many to bury, the survivors had erected a huge funeral pyre and as the flames ignited the entire company said goodbye to the fallen. Already, a few lines of a song about Rope's End Rock had been composed. It would honour them, to ensure that they would never be forgotten.

All had been told of their duties and already some had begun to prepare for departure in the morning. Others would wait, glad that no early start awaited them. The noise from individual groups grew louder as the ale flowed.

A broadhead arrow flew, leaving Eagle-Eye dead in the sand. Men jumped to their feet, dragging weapons into tired hands, seeking the new attackers.

Terryn leaped over a large fallen tree trunk. Others searched for any cover as panic took over.

A young boy emerged from behind a rock, holding a bow of ash. He looked up at the sky with glazed eyes. The shouts of the men failed to raise him from his reverie. Terryn tried to reach him, a long dagger in his hand. On seeing a boy of just ten summers, other warriors stopped him. He had killed one of their own but enough blood had already been spilt, and he was too young to die. Let Lord Bokin decide his fate.

"To answer your previous question of a few hours ago, Lord, it may be some time before the sickness can be cured. For others, maybe it never will," Althalos said.

Lord Bokin saw a cloud of despair descend over Grona's men, blowing around them like cold sleet. He intervened before Terryn and Lowis could cut the boy's throat.

"Take him away. Find his kin. Give him twenty lashes and if the disease still lives inside him, hang him from the rock as a warning to others. And by all the gods, cut down the body of that ranger."

Lord Bokin stood tall, yet inwardly cursed his own actions. A young deranged boy might die by his orders but he knew that he had no choice.

A good man had been killed in a pointless act and his men sought revenge; he would not be deemed weak yet he sincerely hoped that the madness could be thrashed out of him.

The futility of war never failed to disgust him. Too many had died here, most in suicidal attacks against his armed warriors and all due to the savage control of a shaman bent on power. He already loathed this place and vowed to depart as soon as possible, never wanting to see Rope's End Rock again. As the company carried out their chores, the Helgs disappeared into their caves. Most walked but some needed to be carried. With their wits left behind in the dirt of the gorge, they stumbled and limped along. Only the body of the young archer, now swinging in place of the dead ranger, caused a few to look up. The warriors held their heads low, content to be led by wives and children.

Now was the time for Lord Bokin's men to relax, as comrades could swap stories around the fireside and stuff food and drink down waiting throats. Terryn and Lowis had been reunited with Ammett as well as Grona, and all were determined to enjoy the moment. The manner of Eagle-Eye's death had shocked them to the core but they all took the same risks. His memory would never fade as long as good ale disappeared down eager throats.

Grona's tale grew in the telling, until even he failed to remember anything important. Like many others the joy of life shed all their inhibitions.

"All I need is a good whore," Terryn shouted.

"That's all you ever need," Lowis said as he slapped his comrade on the back.

Ammett slowly drank himself into tomorrow's headache. The loss of his good friend Eagle-Eye hurt more than he could bear. Old and weary he lay on his back the loud snoring causing a volley of insults. Lowis covered his body with a blanket and Terryn covered his head.

An unusual quiet descended over the camp as warrior after warrior sank into slumber. Long after that day, the sentries would comment that the men snored like the living but slept like the dead.

Wynne walked into the camp after his stroll in the hills. He knew that Tarn and Grona had both returned safely but his thoughts had led him elsewhere. Could Gisella have been saved all those years ago? Was it his fault that she died? Did Myracadonis have the power to bring her back?

Should he have spared him? Endless questions but he had no answers.

His mind awhirl with torment, he had sat on a jagged rock as if in penance. With no solutions and with darkness all around, he had reluctantly returned to the camp with a headache far worse than any hangover.

On entering Tarn's tent, he knelt by his friend's side, took his hand and kissed it. "I am glad that you live. I would have followed you into the void … but at least your father proved that he does have feelings for you. We all knew what to expect from Grona in the past, but now, he is quiet, secretive, refusing to answer questions. I challenge his motives, as this is unlike him. But I will not leave you again and no harm will come to you from Grona or anyone else. I know that you cannot hear me but I swear on all the gods that my sword will protect you."

The flap of the tent opened and Lord Bokin entered. "Good to see you, Wynne. Next time, do not disobey … no, forget it," he said on seeing the look on Wynne's face. "Get some sleep, man. It is late and we leave early and that … is an order I expect to be carried out."

Wynne rose and departed. As he left the tent, he turned around. "My Lord, this can never happen again."

"I wish that it could be so," Lord Bokin said, so quietly that Wynne struggled to hear him.

"You have made me proud, Captain Tarn. I salute you. Sleep well and know that you are indeed favoured by the gods." Lord Bokin took a long look at Tarn before leaving his tent.

Come the dawn, men with sore heads sat on watered and fed horses awaiting departure. Tarn, although conscious, had been tied to the saddle of a grey mare known for her plodding abilities. Wynne held the reins as well as his own.

The orders given, the company set off for the long trek home. None of them turned to look at the site of so much carnage, leaving only a dust cloud and hoof prints as a reminder of their presence.

In the future heroic songs would be sung, men would remember their fallen comrades, stories would be told – but Rope's End Rock would forever be loathed.

CHAPTER 23

STORMBORN CAVALRY SET an easy pace for a journey that was expected to take between eight and ten days depending on final destinations. The men sat in the tedium of a weary drive, anxious for home and the need to scrub the smell of war from their bodies. But the bad memories would take much longer to be cleansed.

Tarn had recovered sufficiently to ride unfettered by the fourth day. Wynne still rode alongside him, fussing like a mother hen. After two days of near-silence, words began to flow freely between them once more. The big man asked questions but expected little in return. However, Tarn needed to talk. Like a broken dam the words tumbled forth on a wave of relief.

Tarn left nothing out. He had heard Grona's story and thus was able to now fill in most of the missing parts.

"Is that what the gates of Hell are really like?" Wynne asked.

"I didn't really see the gates, only the trail, fence and cross. Perhaps it was due to my vision being blurred by a dense black shadow which surrounded me. Always threatening, I felt that it wanted to suck my body and soul clean."

Wynne frowned, trying, but failing to understand. "How did it feel?"

"It is difficult to explain, so consider this. Some of the Temujin tribes will make an incision in an animal's throat, then hang it to collect the blood in a pail as the beast slowly dies. It is not our way but it is part of their tradition. I'm told the flavour of the meat once cooked is delicious, and chewing made easy on such soft meat. I felt like such a beast. I believed that my life's essence was dripping away."

"But you fought a demon and lived to tell us the story."

"I fought and he died, but I could not survive against the other three with my strength almost spent."

Wynne looked away, his mind flying across the land, trying to picture images of the other world so far removed from the verdant valleys surrounding him. Not for the first time, he silently cursed himself for being unable to stand next to his friend in the abyss. It should not have been his father.

"Do men still talk of my dreams?"

"In any camp there is gossip … but … yes they do," Wynne said.

"Now that my bad dreams have ended perhaps it is time to kill the idle talk. I realise that it was Jade that always judged me, and fairly. Perhaps Tasmina's prayers were answered after all."

Wynne looked away. He had heard Tarn screaming in the night.

"Grona has quietened now we are travelling. There is a change about him, something odd. He failed to take a single drop of ale last night. He is planning something, Tarn, something devious; I know it."

Tarn saw his friend's honest face. Could Grona be changing? And into what? But then he did save me, he thought. Why? There had to be something more to it than Wynne's gut feeling, even though he too had sensed a change in his father's attitude.

"Do you have any meat on the bones Wynne?"

"Not much, but he and his men spend their time poring over maps and stocking up on provisions."

"That could mean anything."

"Maybe Tarn, but their weapons are the first to be sharpened by the armourer, and Grona has ordered the best horse feed from the Temujin. And all questions about their plans are rebuffed."

Tarn pulled gently on the reins, bringing the mare to a stop. He turned and sought Wynne's gaze. "He brought me back. Whatever else he is, he saved my life and I owe him a debt."

"Pah! You owe him nothing. He brought you back because you were there. He would bring anyone back to prove his courage. His boasts had been grating on everyone but this new quiet Grona is a bigger concern. Men are unsure about him; they secretly question his motives. Only his merry men seem unconcerned. They know something." Wynne's anger looked set to bubble over. When he spoke so passionately like this, Tarn realised that perhaps there was a problem; the boil would need to be lanced.

"I will deal with this, Wynne. Just have a little patience."

As they plodded forward Tarn decided to confront his father when the company stopped for the night. One way or another, he had to know.

Eventually Lord Bokin called a halt and the tired company made camp in a pasture beside a lively stream twinkling in the rays of the dying sun. Men turned their noses to the west as the smell of cooking wafted on the breeze. Laughing and joking, the recent sorrows began to be pushed to the furthest corners of their troubled minds. Horses were fed, watered and brushed; some of the soldiers joined with the Temujin, and the chores became simple pleasures. The stench of war began to gradually leach away as some semblance of normality returned.

Tarn and Wynne ate well on salted pork but the mouldy bread needed to be scraped, then toasted. Fresh water cleansed parched throats as they relaxed but an unexpected flagon of extra strong ale, courtesy of Lord Bokin, left a taste of home in their mouths. Tarn had decided to seek out his father after eating but Grona arrived at his tent first. Wynne instantly moved to block his way.

"Hold, big man," Grona said. "I come to speak, to Tarn, nothing else."

Tarn nodded and Wynne walked away. Out of earshot but not out of sight, he sat on a nearby log and watched.

"You look as old as me."

Tarn stayed silent.

"And I doubt you could wield a sword with both hands."

Tarn said nothing.

"Grr! Feeling better?"

"Tired. Now I know how it is to walk in deep mud and be squashed like a fly. Still, you did not come to ask about my health, father."

"Yes and no. I am glad that you are improving but … there are words that must be said." Grona seemed sincere, but too many past insults would not be forgotten after a few kind words. Tarn said nothing.

"Men die in battle, life goes on, that's the way it is. No! Just listen. My life changed in the void. For the better, who knows? But what I do know is that you deserve to learn more of your upbringing and why I left you with my father and mother." With his head turning towards the first star in the sky, Grona hesitated.

"I am big boned and big headed, always have been. From an early age I picked fights with other boys. I rarely lost. As my strength and ability grew, so did my arrogance. Your Grandfather Renda regularly took the strap to me. After a while it didn't hurt. Friends of Renda appeared one day at our home in Lakeside. I insulted one of them over a trivial matter. We fought and although I was beaten, the man lost the sight of his left eye. Your grandfather threw me out. I wandered in despair, taking out my anger on others, yet men joined me. I learned the deadly game of death, fully embracing it as the skills came effortlessly. I sold my sword to the highest bidder."

Tarn tried to interrupt but Grona's hand waved it away.

"These words do not come easy to my tongue, boy ... Tarn. I ask you to listen."

A nod of Tarn's head and his father continued.

"Gods weave magic in strange ways and the meeting of Ellenelle was my dream come true. As willowy as a tender fern in the breeze, her long hair swished around her shoulders taking my breath away. Gentle and kind, she loved everyone, always giving and rarely taking. It took me a long time to win her heart for she had many suitors. Yet your wonderful mother ruled me with a steely determination. I never won an argument and for a while my life changed. Then you were born and old habits die hard."

"And you left," Tarn said with bitterness.

"Yes. Your crying kept me awake and I hated the smell of baby milk and shit in equal measure. The big world outside called me – come and live, it said. Convincing myself that others needed me more than my own family, I left on a pretext. I can't even remember what it was. Thus I wandered and became a mercenary once again – the easy option. I returned regularly, or as often as I could, and your wonderful mother, my Ellenelle, always forgave. She knew that my world was so much larger than our small house and that I was the master of my own destiny. I never heard her raise her voice or try to persuade me to stay, yet the sorrow in her eyes will haunt me forever. Over the years I saw you grow and recognised not my son, but a new version of my own father, dear Renda. I hated him, so began to hate you."

"You did not have to hate. Did you ever think of me? How much I worshipped my heroic father fighting battles to save us all. When I was small, mother told me stories of you and only you. I yearned to be like you, even trying to act like you. All I ever wanted was a father to love me but you failed, over and over again. Before mother passed away she prayed every day for you, but you never returned."

Grona ran his hands through his hair. "I have not come to apologise, for I am what I am, but … it is sad that we are not close. If I could change that I would."

"Why did you leave when mother died? I needed you more than ever then."

Tired eyes misted over as Grona fought to control his emotions. His thoughts raced back to the breech birth, the blood and cold bodies of wife and daughter. He had arrived an hour after her demise feeling utterly helpless for the first time in his life.

"Because my father ordered me to leave. He and mother Sollos declared that they would take care of you, thus ensuring that you would never become like me. Deep inside I knew that both of them spoke truly yet my pride overruled that notion. As my loathing of him grew so it did whenever I saw you. Your eyes always seemed so judgemental."

"Yes they were, but could you not also see the longing, the need to be accepted by my own father? I had lost my mother, and my father wanted nothing to do with me. Is it any wonder that as I grew into manhood, my eyes sought yours for some sign of recognition? It took me a long time to learn how, and when to give up on a lost cause." Tarn laid his hands on the side of the tent, as if trying to push away his rising anger. "I hated you."

"How can I blame you? For over the years I did everything that I could to undermine you. Yet begrudgingly I realised that you had grown into a strong and fair man, no doubt due to your mother's early influence, but jealously is a powerful emotion and I had enough for ten men."

Tarn immediately countered. "Did you not think me reckless, like you, when I charged the Helgs in the last battle near Castle Bokin? That was not my mother fighting. I wanted to be like you and I fought like you. Grandfather Renda taught me, but your fighting skills inspired me. Why did you hate me so much afterwards?"

"Because you triumphed. You achieved the victory that I craved. You collected the gold and the land, but most of all you received the glory and the respect."

As both men paused for breath, they could see many soldiers staring at them due to their raised voices. Wynne had stood, looking intently at them. He sat down once more.

"Why did you save me?"

With a smile, Grona turned his head to look elsewhere. "To tell you the truth, I did not know where you went. A nagging female voice in my head pressed me to leap into the Horned Demon and although I believed I could withstand the persistent sound … I wanted to kill that bastard one way or another." He paused to look directly at his son. "In the dark … well, I am glad that I heard your voice."

"A truthful answer, father – are you changing?"

"Perhaps, but only time will tell. In the morning my men and I will leave the company. It is time."

"I have heard rumours of maps, sharpened swords and horse feed." Tarn said.

"For once the camp gossip, is true. Yet I plead innocence of plans against anyone in this camp," Grona chuckled.

"Where will you go?"

Grona paused, recalling memories of his battles. A good question, he thought. I could lie but conversely I could tell the truth.

"I will lead my men where the money is. Mercenaries are always wanted at Fisher Port and the Seafarers are happy to provide safe passage. If the rumours are correct then the Southern Lands are so full of treasure that if we liberate a piece here and there, no one will miss it. Anyway, the whorehouses are supposed to offer delights unknown to us starved men in the north." Grona had closed his eyes but his face showed that he was already travelling. A new world enticed him, the bodies of lithe girls seduced him. "Or maybe not … perhaps we can revisit the east. Turlo has forever welcomed us. The harlots may not be as talented as those in the south but I guarantee they don't cost as much. And I do understand what they are saying." A good laugh, a deep booming laugh rose from his chest. As a slight redness flushed his cheeks, Grona grinned.

Tarn stood up. "We are kin; you are welcome at my house, father."

Taken aback, Grona looked for any ambiguity in Tarn's voice yet he found none. "I would dearly love to see my granddaughter."

"So you should. Not only has it been too long, but she is the image of my mother."

The shock hit home as the face of his beloved Ellenelle flashed into his brain. Pangs of guilt followed. Grona put both large hands to his mouth, rubbing fingers on a weathered nose.

"I never knew."

"Now you do."

Tarn extended his right hand and his father took it in his own. Neither wanted to break the hold. "Twice in a few days, this could become habit-forming, son," Grona said.

He turned and slowly walked away, a spring in his step and a wide smile on his face. On returning to his men Terryn mocked. "Found us some gold, have we?"

"No ... but maybe I have."

CHAPTER 24

BY THE TIME Tarn had risen the next morning, Grona and his band had already left, as had the Temujin. More parting would follow. King Leofrick had ridden in with Stormborn troops to collect the body of his son and heir. They would head south and return to Castle Stoke as soon as possible. Lord Bokin would lead the Maxilla men back to the east and home.

Many friendships had been forged and promises of future meetings made. United in battle, and tied by the bonds of sharing in adversity, the men bade each other farewell, happy to be returning home.

The two leaders had jointly agreed to hold a celebration six months hence in the fields around Castle Bokin. The dead would be formally honoured and all would be invited.

The last journey home awaited.

Wynne and Tarn chattered away the miles over the next three days.

As they crested the final hill and looked down on Lakeland and the Wide Lake, they patted each other on the back. Raucous cheers from all the Bokin men broke the silence; even the horses snorted. All took in the pure air, the exhilaration intoxicating as the company separated.

Saddle-sore but glad to be back, the berserk warrior and the shaman killer gently urged their steeds forward. With the lake shimmering in the sunshine behind Tarn's house, the two warriors clasped each other's wrists.

"See you in the morning," Tarn said.

"I doubt that," Wynne replied with a massive grin as he rode away.

As he stood before the heavy oak door, Tarn read the inscription that he had lovingly carved: 'Enter and be Welcome'.

He also saw the sheaves of arrows, bows and daggers neatly stacked outside. He smiled. Wondering what his wife had been up to, he knew that Tasmina, was never going to be unprepared for anything.

A lift of the latch, a solid push and the familiarity of his home swept over him in a wave of love.

Tasmina sat on a stool, her back to the door, as she combed her long shiny hair. Her scent wafted towards him and sent his pulse racing. She had dressed herself in a flowing robe of white cotton, tied at the waist with a yellow ribbon. As she turned, a wondrous smile appeared; she had never looked more beautiful. Tarn gaped, his eyes a mixture of love and relief.

One step then two and she wrapped her sensuous body around him, hair as black as night cascading over his face. Smothered with kisses, Tarn found it difficult to breathe so he simply held on. Letting his beautiful wife go was the last thing on his mind. Eventually she pulled away, fire in her eyes.

"So! Home at last are we? You think me idle after all these weeks away. You wouldn't believe how busy I've been and how little I've missed you. Lori has almost forgotten her father and I nearly took a lover to warm my bed on these cold nights."

"And where is my beautiful daughter?" he asked.

"With friends. I had a message an hour ago that you would soon be home," she whispered in his ear.

A mischievous smile spread across her face as she reached for Tarn again. Crushing her breasts into his wide chest, she began to purr very softly.

"What are you singing?"

"Foolish man. I am wishing … wishing on a distant star, the one I call Jade."

"What are you wishing for?"

"One day I will tell you, my husband."

Tarn rolled his eyes as a wave of tiredness washed over him. "I need to sleep for a week," he said.

"Sleep? You can sleep later husband. Now I am going to show you what you have been missing these past weeks, and you can fulfil the promise that you made," Tasmina said as she led him into the back bedroom.

CHAPTER 25

MYRACADONIS FOUND HIMSELF in a world of pain. He remembered Wynne's killing stroke but nothing else as he awoke on a mass of slithering shapes. Fangs struck his body as the snakes tried to coil around his arms. The land shuddered under his feet as he desperately fought to pull himself upright. Dark shapes flew past, indistinct but menacing. A large cat hissed at him, baring its teeth. Spiders crawled up his legs, leaving a trail of his blood as they moved ever closer towards his groin.

He looked up to the sky, seeking salvation from the gods, but he could only see evil shapes lurking in the darkness. He heard the howls of tormented creatures and the claps of thunder from an approaching cyclone. A violet flash and a lightning strike turned his night to day. Something threw a black shadow over him as it passed above. Following the flight he watched as a large crow flew around in decreasing circles. When a thick post appeared out of the gloom it landed.

"Your life is forfeit, Myracadonis. There are many that wish revenge but I doubt that now they will have the opportunity where you are going. I am the gatekeeper and I see many lost souls in this unforgiving place. Here they suffer, but alas, you are destined to endure everlasting torment at the hands of the demons. They are coming and the gates of Hell will open. Prepare yourself."

Myracadonis stared into the mists, his eyes bulging forward. Screams carried on the wind making his body tremble. He attempted to walk away as the sound of a large animal padded towards him, but trying to lift his feet from the putrescent filth proved impossible. Red eyes glowed in the dark. A two headed wolf appeared. Pieces of flesh fell to the ground as the mouths gaped; the fangs dripping with saliva and claret. A pack of hounds followed the wolf, spreading out to surround him.

A gate opened. The stench of evil hit him like a hammer blow. Fireballs exploded in the land of Hell as bats flew out to attack him. As the demons grabbed his body and pulled him through the gates, Myracacdonis tried to move ... but he couldn't even scream.

THE END

EPILOGUE

THE GREAT CAVERN, open to the skies, had seldom held such a gathering of all the gods as well as lesser deities. Huge chairs of white marble etched with wild beasts and demons had been created as a sign of opulence. The gods sat in rows above their inferiors, whilst Obsidian the Dark God and his wife Radiance, the Goddess of Light and Air, sat above them all. The destiny of the planet usually rested with their decisions, but sometimes, when the gods tired, mortals would be allowed to rule for a while.

With a fanfare of trumpets the King and Queen took their seats – thrones made of ivory and covered in the down of a million songbirds. Lavish silk footstools appeared at their feet. The silence grew as the sprites of King and Queen sought those in need of chastisement. No one dared breathe or move.

The Goddess of Light and Air, was worshipped by many lesser beings. Their vision of a women, wise beyond all others, was close to the truth. Radiance left beauty to her daughters, as she preferred a kindly face and a warm persona. But not today.

She rose, her long robes trailing behind. She looked at her family, her face threatening.

"As usual, you have behaved appallingly, my children. But this time you have gone too far. Mankind has suffered grievously. They need a lengthy period to recover from their losses and the heartache of so much suffering. The war has ended; let them mourn their dead. But yet again I would remind you of their mortality. Too many have died because of two wars in a single human decade. I should not have to remind you that human babies are not grown on trees – they are conceived. They need to repopulate many regions of their lands and that takes time. I am disappointed in you for allowing too many to die. If the war had continued, centuries would elapse before the population could return to previous levels. As it stands, decades will pass. Being the true gods we have a duty to manipulate mankind as we see fit, but never to eradicate them from this world. There will be no more games until I give my permission."

"As you wish, Mother," Titian said, lounging on a slab of quartz that he had created. Radiance saw his mind racing, hating her chastisement. Good, she thought to herself, he may feel secure but I know all his weaknesses.

Radiance sought the eye of her daughter Jade, the Earth Goddess of Love, Peace and Harmony. She saw her daughter's concern and nodded in agreement.

This scene had been enacted over and over since the beginning of time. They all knew the correct rites. If humans were not to vanish completely then a short period must pass. Months, years; the gods cared little. To them the seasons would pass in the blink of an eye.

The Dark God had listened to the words of his wife, whilst trying to probe the minds of their offspring. A raging fury was threatening to erupt as he saw few signs of total compliance from some of them. Obsidian rose to hover above his family, his robes changing to the colour of his name, his hands holding a slender sword.

"Your mother is correct and you *will* obey her this time. Our influence would wane, possibly vanish altogether if the race of man was ever wiped from this planet. Our power grows when they flourish. The more babies they produce, the more you can punish, corrupt, misuse, shelter or even love. Humans are tested every day by the gods. This premise must never be placed at risk by any of you. Any transgression will be severely punished. You have been warned."

Obsidian looked around. His children tried to keep their minds closed; most failed. Secrets were never secrets for too long. All he had to do was push harder.

"Titian, would you like another trip to Hell? I seem to remember a docile son after your last visit."

The God of Fire chose his words carefully. "Naturally, I agree with you both. I am sure that my beloved sisters and brothers feel the same way. If the game of war created such chaos, I apologise. If man has to repopulate some areas, I am mortified. And if, Father, you think that I would ever deliberately disobey you, then I am horrified. Our power will grow and we will continue to flourish. Dear Mother and Father, as ever I am yours to command."

Obsidian considered his son's words. He looked into his eyes and saw disobedience. If you think that you won't get caught next time, think again Titian. You will never win, no matter how hard you try.

"Good! In time I am sure that you can find another human only too eager to control his own kind. For now, I want all of you to ensure that the next years are kind, that the crops flourish and humans prosper. Make them happy for our sake. As the true gods it is our responsibility."

"And mine is to sow the seeds of discontent for war," Titian said softly to his sister Jade.

RICK HAYNES

ABOUT THE AUTHOR

Laughter - the best medicine in the world
Reading and writing - the best pastime

I believe in having fun and enjoying myself, as life is far too short to do anything else. I have a real eclectic taste and can be found writing wonderful Drabbles – stories of just 100 words – as well as short and longer stories and all in differing genres.

But a tale of fantasy can go a long, long way. If you like my work then all the effort is worthwhile.

My Motto:

LAUGH LOUD - LOVE ALWAYS - LIVE LONG

http://profnexus.wix.com/rickhaynes
https://www.facebook.com/rick.haynes.9028

FUTURE PROJECTS

Heroes Never Fade will be the second in the Maxilla series.

I am currently preparing the outline for this, my follow-up novel, which is planned for release in early 2016.

My granddaughter wishes to collaborate with me in writing a collection of fairy tales. This project, together with a collection of Christmas stories, should be available within the next twelve months.

Made in the USA
Charleston, SC
24 July 2015